BETWEEN SISTERS

BETWEEN SISTERS

•

ADWOA BADOE

GROUNDWOOD BOOKS
HOUSE OF ANANSI PRESS
TORONTO / BERKELEY

The writer would like to acknowledge the financial assistance of the Ontario Arts Council, which is an agency of the Government of Ontario.

Groundwood Books/House of Anansi Press
110 Spadina Avenue, Suite 801, Toronto, Ontario M5V 2K4
or c/o Publishers Group West
1700 Fourth Street, Berkeley, CA 94710

We acknowledge for their financial support of our publishing program the Canada Council for the Arts, the Government of Canada through the Canada Book Fund (CBF) and the Ontario Arts Council.

Canada Council   Conseil des Arts
for the Arts   du Canada

ONTARIO ARTS COUNCIL
CONSEIL DES ARTS DE L'ONTARIO

Library and Archives Canada Cataloguing in Publication
Badoe, Adwoa
Between sisters / Adwoa Badoe.
ISBN 978-0-88899-996-2 (bound).–ISBN 978-0-88899-997-9 (pbk.)
I. Title.
PS8553.A312B47 2010   jC813'.54   C2010-901682-3

Cover photograph: © Mimi Mollica/Corbis
Design by Michael Solomon

Groundwood Books is committed to protecting our natural environment.
As part of our efforts, this book is printed on paper that contains 100%
post-consumer recycled fibers, is acid-free and is processed chlorine-free.

Printed and bound in Canada

For Victoria

If we can walk, we can dance.
— African proverb

• ONE •

Not'ing wonders God.

This is what my daa says when something unexpected happens to take the wind out of his belly. Apparently things like that happen often in life, because I have heard him say those words over and over again.

Friday June 3 began strangely because we woke up to water running freely in our standing pipe after a year of silence, when the mains in our neighborhood of Alajo were shut down. A burst pipeline, somebody said, and the faucet became indifferent whichever way we twisted the tap.

Then we forgot what the tap was for until I heard Effie screaming in my ear.

"Gloria, wake up!"

"Hmmmm?" I was losing my dream. We were out playing in the field...

Effie shook me, and I had to open my eyes.

I opened the right one first. The left one felt as though someone had poured starch over it to glue it shut. Sleep struggled to keep its hold on me.

"Sit up," she commanded.

I did so, ever so slowly dragging my legs over the side of the bed. I had gone to sleep after midnight because I had attended the Thursday prayer meeting with Daa and we had much to pray about: Maa's health, a job for Daa, a vocation for me, and Effie's attitude.

But the day had come too soon. Not because the sun rose to ruffle the neck feathers of our neighbor's cockerel, but because all of sudden, just like that, the water gushed out of the standing pipe and splashed on the circle of concrete where we placed our buckets.

Apparently James Adama, the cobbler who lived in the third apartment in the house, woke up first.

"Water," he shouted in spite of the hour. It was four-thirty in the morning.

Eno and Asibi, two sisters who lived in the second apartment, woke up, too. Daa woke up and shouted for us. And now Effie was doing her best to get me out of bed.

Soon we were scrambling for every container we could find to fill with precious water.

"Fetch the gallon beneath the table. Empty the rubber filled with oranges. Don't forget to fill the cooler," Maa said, pointing to our red clay water pot.

We even filled the empty beer bottles. We could not trust that the water would continue to flow through the tap in our compound, even for the rest of the day. It was easier to trust the twenty-minute walk to the Caprice Hotel, where we usually fetched our water in aluminum buckets that we carried on our heads, balanced on soft rolls of cloth.

Today Effie and I would be spared the evening walk and the crick in our necks, but our job was no easier now as we lined up behind our housemates and fetched container after container of water.

Breakfast was a thick slice of sugar bread with a dab of Blue Band margarine, which I munched on my way to school, joining my friends along the road. Buses and taxis were revving their engines, overfilling with workers and screeching threadbare tires against the tar. Porridge and koose sellers mingled with beggars. Every now and then a squawking car horn alerted us to the danger of walking too close to the road.

Effie had left for her catering school minutes before me. Maa would go to her shared stall at the Mallam Atta Market. I could only guess at what Daa would do all day until we returned to our three rooms in our shared compound house, the place we called home.

The sun shone brightly on my neighborhood school. Our cream and brown uniforms had been ordered by the government for every school child in the country. Too bad they did not order our shoes as well. There was every kind of footwear, from slippers to boots in every color. A few people wore their socks pulled high or rolled over at their ankles. Even if some people wore shoes with holes in their soles, nobody was barefooted. Mr. Jonas the headmaster insisted on that.

"God bless our homeland, Ghana! And make our nation great and strong," four hundred voices sang boldly to the wind and the trees in our school compound.

We were lined up in eighteen long columns in front of the great veranda at the Alajo Number Five Experimental Elementary and Junior Secondary School for the morning assembly. Each class was represented by two columns of about twenty students each. My class, being the most senior, was at the extreme left, and we stood one behind another sweating in the sun. I tried to remember when my class had lined up at the extreme right when I was just beginning school.

Next there were the announcements. Mr. Jonas was speaking in his nasally accented English, which was hard to understand. In school everyone said he was too "colo" — old-fashioned. Every other male teacher wore regular black trousers and a shirt, but Mr. Jonas wore his white shirt tucked into starched khaki shorts, and long white socks up to his knees.

We were fidgety while he spoke until he said, "The results of this year's JSS exams are in and will be posted on the notice board in the office."

Something in my chest dropped in my belly — pom! I lost the rest of the headmaster's comments and I didn't even hear the words of the pledge we recited just before each class marched to their classroom.

The dreaded day had come, and all I could hope for was a miracle. I had never done well in school, not even when I repeated class six, just before I came to JSS. My problem was reading. My problem was just about everything, really.

I felt dizzy. I felt I would lose the sugar bread in my

belly if I so much as spoke. I found my chair and sat down behind my desk. Miss Tanoh calmed the class down and called us in groups of twelve to go to the office to view the results. My name, Gloria Bampo, meant that I would be in the very first group.

"Nii Tetteh Addo, Kofi Andah, Gloria Bampo..." she called, checking our names off a list.

We made a single file and walked up the corridor toward the office. In our school we filed for everything!

We crowded around the notice board searching for our names. I held back, almost too afraid to look.

There was my name, third on the list. I was the first to fail. Out of fifteen subjects I had failed thirteen, passing only needlework and art.

A river welled up in my tight chest. Last again! How could I return to the classroom? How would I hold back my tears? How would I survive the day?

The answer was simple. I would spend the day locked in a toilet cubicle.

I rushed off while the others celebrated with explosions of high fives.

The girls' toilet was not the best place to be. Too busy, too smelly and too dirty. The good thing was my tears dried quickly. I blew my nose hard and I walked back to the classroom. God must have made me invisible because nobody took any notice of me in my corner, as people pondered what all those numbers meant for their future opportunities.

I did not remain invisible the whole day. Soon the

news spread that some of us had failed. Some of us had failed badly! Naa Koshie didn't care. Her mother, who lived in England, was going to return for her. She even had a passport.

"After all, I passed English," she laughed. "That's all I'm going to need in England!"

I wished I had something defiant to say. I had nothing. My best friends, Janet and Afi, stayed with me during recreation. But it was sad company. They had nothing to say. They had passed and I could tell they were bursting to celebrate.

That was the first time I spoke those words, "Not'ing wonders God." Right then I understood my daa. I understood defeat.

What would Effie say? What would Maa and Daa say?

Then the bell rang to close school for the day. I left my friends behind.

Along the way home, I decided to say nothing about my results until I had a plan. I pushed back my shoulders and increased my pace. For one month I had been an Ananse Guide, when it had been offered free to every girl in our school. I joined for just long enough to be taught to march straight.

As I walked, I even tried to sing a praise song, but my throat closed up over the words. All that escaped was a loud hiccup. I took the long path home.

•

It is easy to think with a tray of oranges balanced on one's head, especially when it is done day after day for five years. Carrying oranges was far easier than carrying water, even if one had to walk for several hours, peddling fruit. Normally I would have waited for Janet and Afi, who peddled bananas and groundnuts, the poor man's dinner. Oranges were the cheap control for thirst until water began to show up in plastic bags at every street corner. We had to walk longer then to sell everything.

I wandered from one street to the next, forgetting to shout my wares. I wanted to think. I wanted time to deal with my shame and sorrow so that I could trust myself not to cry salt-tears when I faced my parents. Most of all I needed a solution to Gloria Bampo's hope-starved future.

A woman walked by holding a large black handbag and smelling of Zenata perfume. She greeted me as she passed.

I thought of Auntie Ruby, who always smelled of Zenata. For two months she had been visiting Maa with plans of taking me as a nanny for one of her relatives. Maa always said I was still in school.

I had several friends who lived with aunts and other relatives as house maids. Their lives always seemed hard, not only because of the amount of work they did but because of the stories they told of the wickedness done to them in those homes — rough speaking, beatings and name-calling.

I had said to Maa that I would rather sell medicinal herbs with her at the smelly market than become a maid. I would even travel with her across the country to Togo or Ivory Coast to trade.

But she'd laughed softly and said, "You don't know what you're saying. You are only a child."

I found a path that wound around the backyards of some of the larger houses, those ones that were surrounded by high walls, once white but now stained a dirty brown. The tall grass scratched at my legs.

Did Maa have to push through bushes like these when she went selling across country? Probably worse, I imagined. This was the city.

"Akutu wula, akutu wula!"

The sharp call pierced through my thoughts. A man was calling for the orange seller. He was calling for me.

"Yes," I replied.

"Are you deaf or daydreaming?" He was standing at the door of the boys' quarters of a bungalow. I couldn't tell if he was angry or joking, so I said nothing. I went toward him as he was making no attempt to come to me. I had sold nothing up until then. What would Maa say about that?

I lifted the tray off my head.

"Put it on this table," he commanded, pointing to a table on his veranda.

I did so. I watched him. He didn't smile. His eyes were red, his manner sour and there it was, the unmistakable smell of akpeteshie booze. He spoke in a mixture of Ga and English.

"*Ene*, how much?" he demanded. I began to explain the prices according to size.

"This one here is 200 cedis for one and that one is 300 cedis. I have already peeled some," I said, pointing to the smaller oranges.

"Give me two," he commanded.

I picked them up and as I stretched my hand toward him, he grasped my wrist and pulled me down. His grip was strong, even painful.

I screamed before I knew what was happening. Quick as a cat I twisted out of his grasp and was on my feet and running.

"Hey, *akutu wula*," he shouted after me. "*Mini sane, buulu?* Come back, fool!"

I didn't look back. I left my tray behind with all the oranges and the knife, too. If it was a theft, he had succeeded. If it was a rape, I had escaped.

It was only then that I realized how late it was, for the last of the orange streaks had left the evening sky, and gray was giving way to indigo.

Where was I? I kept running and running.

Then there was Daavi, our kelewele seller sitting atop her stool, fanning the early fire on our familiar street corner.

Here I was, home again.

Not'ing wonders God!

• TWO •

Maa said I had been foolish to go by myself to sell oranges. She wanted to know why, so I told them about my failed JSS exam.

"Oh, Gloria," she sighed.

"Not'ing wonders God," Daa muttered.

The next morning, Maa sent Daa with me to that man's house to retrieve my oranges and my tray. With my heart pounding, we went searching in the suburb, but my memory was confused and I couldn't find the house.

Daa thought I was telling lies.

"Gloria, *whe yie-o*. It is your future we're fighting for. Don't give the devil a chance. He is only too pleased to take whatever you offer him."

"But, Daa, I haven't done anything."

He raised a cautioning finger. "I wasn't born yesterday."

Maa was too angry to say anything when we got home. Only Effie believed me.

That afternoon, Effie and I ate ampesi and agushie stew from the same bowl. The plantains were soft and the stew was pepper-hot and well salted. Effie and I shared a piece of fried fish evenly.

"Gloria, you have to take the test again and pass even if you have to cheat," Effie said. "Otherwise you will remain just an ignorant kurasi-ni, and you'll have to do dirty jobs like Eno and Asibi, or Maa."

Right then my fears formed a clear picture of doom, and I said, "Effie, God is good. God will show a way."

I wished my faith was as strong as my words.

"Oh, Gloria, don't be like Daa," Effie said with a sigh.

I didn't answer. Daa blamed malevolent abayifo for everything that went wrong in his life. It was for this reason that he had thrown himself into prayer, fighting all the evil forces that worked against him.

"How will you get an education with no passes and no money? Hm?" Effie demanded in fierce whispers.

"God has a way."

Effie sighed. "Oh, Gloria, you're doubly in trouble. As for me, I choose to be practical."

Effie had changed since she had begun to study catering at the Dufleur establishment in town. Daa railed against her for the diligence she took with her lipstick and eyeshadow each day.

"If you had spent as much time and effort on your studies, Effie Bampo, you would have won scholarships for your senior secondary," he would say. "Instead you've given up good brains for paint!"

Daa had something against make-up. He had something against fashion.

More and more, Effie didn't care what Daa thought. But she still had to obey him and go to our Saturday youth meetings at church.

•

Brother Divine stood at the front of the youth room of the Alajo Pentecostal Church. Two pairs of fluorescent light tubes bathed the room with white light. Behind him, four boys sat behind musical instruments: an electric piano, a set of drums, a bass guitar and an electric guitar. He led the praises with eyes closed and head tilted up toward heaven.

He liked his songs slow and meaningful, the lyrics drawn out. We sang along with him.

"Everything is subject to change. Everything." Brother Divine's voice cut through my thoughts like a langalanga knife through thick grass.

I wanted to believe that everything would change, that suddenly I would receive a letter from the Examination Council saying they had made a mistake and that I had actually passed. Then come September I would be heading off to Accra Polytechnic to study fashion and dressmaking.

Brother Divine spoke on the topic of hope. We prayed for the needy to have jobs, schools, healing, visas and money. Many of us received words of encouragement. Some broke down weeping. I began to feel hopeful. But through all this, Effie leafed through a magazine, unconcerned.

Effie and I walked with Akos, Sofia and Kofi Dapaah.

Around us other groups formed as people made their way home. Our chatter and laughter carried though the night.

A red Mitsubishi saloon car stopped some distance ahead of us, hazard lights flashing. A sharp blast of the horn was followed by a shout — "Effie!"

"Who is it?" I asked. Perhaps someone was going to give us a ride home.

A look passed between Sofia and Effie. Then Effie said, "Gloria, wait for me at the kelewele curb, okay?"

"Where are you going?" I asked.

"Nowhere."

"Effie," I shouted. But she laughed and ran off with Sofia in tow.

"Just wait for me, okay?" she yelled. And they were gone.

Akos and Kofi walked on with me. Akos was in her final senior secondary year, and Kofi was studying to become a guild certified electrician.

A small group of people had gathered by the popular kelewele stand. Kofi had some money, and so we waited while he bought kelewele.

From her low stool by the fire, Daavi stirred the large pan of frying plantains. Then she turned to her customers, counting spicy plantains into squares of old newspaper.

"Look, I'm giving you extra for the sake of friendship," she said, dropping in four or five more small pieces. We thanked her profusely. Then we all sat there on the curb and ate together.

It was dark, but the flames from Daavi's open fire gave us light, along with the headlights of the few cars that snorted down our narrow street.

"I hope Effie comes soon," I said.

"Sofia has found Effie a boyfriend," said Akos.

"Oh," I gasped. "Daa is against us having boyfriends."

Kofi rolled the greasy newspaper wrapper into a ball and threw it into Daavi's fire. We watched it burn.

"Don't worry, she'll be fine," he said. "Effie is smart."

"So long as she's careful," said Akos. "I agree with Brother Divine. I don't want any boyfriend problems. I want to finish school well."

"Who is her boyfriend?" I asked.

"He is a seaman," said Akos.

"Seamen are very generous," said Kofi, laughing.

"Seamen are also notorious for having many girl-friends," Akos retorted.

I heard a dog howling from afar. Then all the other neighborhood dogs began to howl, too. Perhaps a ghost was passing.

"Unlike some of you, I have guild exams to write," Kofi said. Then he left.

Akos waited with me, but half an hour later there was still no sign of Effie.

"I'm going home, too," said Akos.

I sat by myself on the curb by Daavi, unable to go home to answer questions about Effie. I scratched the mosquito bites on my legs and wondered why Effie no longer shared her secrets with me.

• THREE •

"Auntie Ruby is here. She's asking for you," said Effie, opening the door to our room.

I stretched and let out a great yawn. Effie wrinkled her face at my morning breath but I ignored her. There was no reason for me to wake up early anymore.

The week after the publishing of the JSS results was painful. I had never felt so stupid in my life. I felt as if everyone was talking about me behind my back. Even my friends seemed to lapse into silence whenever they saw me. I feigned a stomach ache and missed the special celebration at school. I wasn't getting any prizes and I didn't want to be remembered in any photos. Then I dropped out of school altogether.

"Maa told me to get you," Effie said.

"Is she feeling better?"

"Yes," she replied. Maa's coughing had been terrible during the night.

My dress hung on the back of the only chair in our room. I took off the faded T-shirt that passed for a nightie and reached for my dress. I pulled it quickly over my head.

"Gloria, wear a bra!" Effie said.

I hated the way she called my name when she was bossing me around.

I dragged the dress over my head. It was my favorite linen dress, bright yellow with rows of silver embroidery covering the neck and two large pockets. I loved to sink my hands deep into the pockets when I was standing with nothing to do.

I groped for the pail beneath my bed and took out my toothbrush and paste. I stopped on the veranda to scoop some water from the huge barrel we kept outside our room. Our standing pipe had died again and we had returned to fetching water from the hotel.

I crossed the compound to the bath house, washed my face from the tiny pail and brushed my teeth, spitting into the gutter. Globs of foamy toothpaste floated into the large drain.

I wrinkled my nose. No matter how often we scrubbed the bath house, I couldn't stand the smell of wastewater stagnating inside the concrete-lined drains. In school my teacher had taught us about bacteria. I imagined millions of them growing in the gutter, feeding on toothpaste and early-morning-mouth sourness.

On the other veranda, Eno and Asibi were cracking palm nuts with stones, filling a large white enamel basin with palm kernels. The two women traded in palm nuts and palm oil. Their clothes were always heavily stained, and they smelled of smoke and burnt oil. They looked as dirty as the garage mechanics who spent their days beneath broken-down cars in the lot, rubbing their clothes in dirt and grease.

I could never do a job like that, I thought. Yet Effie had said that I could end up like Eno and Asibi.

I was clear eyed, fresh mouthed and moving more quickly. The sun was up, the day was bright and the flies were buzzing around, giddy from the heat. On our aging concrete wall, red-headed lizards sunned themselves.

I opened the door to the living room and found my mother sitting with Auntie Ruby.

"My dear," said Auntie Ruby. She laughed, and her eyes crinkled at the corners. Auntie Ruby was always happy. "Come, my friend. I hope you're not sick to be sleeping so late, hm?"

I had just enough time to shake my head before she was up on her feet and coming toward me. Her large arms circled me in a big hug. She smelled of Zenata and camphor. I could imagine hundreds of those little white camphor balls in her clothes trunk, deterring cockroaches from laying eggs around her bubus and kabaslits.

For a short while I suffocated in her embrace. At last she pushed me back, keeping her hands on my shoulders.

"You're growing like Acheampong weed," she said, delighted. "Every time I see you, you're that much taller." She raised an upturned hand to show me just how fast I was growing.

"Yes, she's growing quickly but not as resistant as Acheampong, I hope," said Maa. It was good to hear the humor in her soft voice. The lines on her forehead were less harsh when her eyes smiled.

I thought about those weeds that grew carelessly in the bush, so tough to cut down that Ghanaians had named them after an ex-military head of state. I laughed.

My mother looked on, smiling. She wasn't the kind who spoke much. She just went about her life, cleaning and cooking when she was home. When she wasn't at home, she was dealing in traditional healing herbs made from bark and leaves — the kind they soaked in alcoholic bitters or mashed with ash and water to heal fractures, skin diseases, infertility, paralysis and headaches. Effie said it was impossible for one mixture to cure everything, but Maa said black-people knowledge was different from white-people knowledge. White-people knowledge was in books, but our wise men and women were privy to the speech of the plants.

"So, what's happening with you?" Auntie Ruby asked. She patted the arm of the red armchair, and I went over and sat down.

Our living room was small and crowded. There were two armchairs that stood opposite each other on either side of the green loveseat. Three side tables filled in the gaps between chairs, and a coffee table occupied the center of the room. The rest of the space was taken by a large cupboard where all the plates and cups were kept.

With each passing Harmattan season, more of the plywood surfaces lifted off the tables at the edges. In frustration Effie had stripped the surfaces completely off two of the side tables, leaving unvarnished wood.

A musky scent came from the old thick curtains and the threadbare armchairs that we had owned as long as I could remember.

"I have finished JSS," I said.

"With distinction, I hope."

I grimaced. I was sixteen, and yet I could barely read.

"So what are your plans?" Auntie Ruby asked. "Which school did you choose for SSS?"

"I'm not going to SSS. I want to learn to sew." I hoped I sounded confident.

"You'd make a good seamstress," Auntie Ruby said. "You have style."

I smiled. What I really wanted to do was sing highlife. But when I had confided in my daa, he'd replied, "Nonsense. If you want to sing, join the church choir."

My father took his position as church elder as seriously as he'd taken his driving career. Once upon a time he had chauffeured important people in our government. He boasted of meeting foreign heads of states. "Robert Mugabe of Zimbabwe, Mobutu Seseku of Zaire, Houphoët-Boigny of Ivory Coast and Sékou Touré of Guinea — I drove them all," he would say, checking them off his fingers. And his eyes would light up.

Two and a half years ago, he lost his job driving the secretary for information. Effie said that Daa had dropped off the minister at a state function and then wandered off with the minister's car on his own errand. He had kept his boss waiting at the end of the function. They gave him the sack right away.

Since then, Daa had found church in a big way. He was there so often, they put him in charge of visiting the sick. Effie said he might as well have been called into the priesthood. At least then he would be paid for all his devotion.

Although Daa's unemployment frustrated us all, I didn't like it when Effie spoke badly of him. He was trying and at least, unlike Eno's husband, he had not abandoned us. And unlike James the cobbler, Daa did not drink.

So I joined the church choir as Daa suggested. But I'd noticed that although everyone considered highlife singing a poor choice for a career, everyone had their radios tuned to Radio One all the time. We sang along when the songs of Daddy Lumba and Nana Tuffuor and all the other stars were played on the radio. I even caught Daa humming along.

But when people asked me what I wanted to do now, I said I wanted to sew. I loved clothes, too. I knew the latest fashions, and sometimes I changed some of the clothes we bought at Auntie Ruby's second-hand clothing shop to make them more fashionable. But we had to watch what we wore around Daa. He hated thin straps and bareback dresses. He hated high-riding slits along the sides of our skirts.

"The trouble with today's world is licentiousness," he would say with disgust. "Small-small girls are looking for sugar daddies to feed off! Gloria, Effie, don't become like one of them. Money is the root of all evil."

Effie and I laughed at this, though of course we did not dare laugh to his face.

"Gloria, Auntie Ruby wants you to meet her cousin who has just come from England and is looking for someone to help with minding her baby." It was my mother speaking.

"Christy is a doctor and she's so generous. That girl is an angel," Auntie Ruby declared. "She won't treat you harshly and I know she'll sponsor you through sewing school. If I'd had someone like her to raise me, I would have ended up Somebody."

Life seemed to be made up of Somebodies and Nobodies. Auntie Ruby looked like a Somebody, in her flowing burgundy bubu and huge Anago head tie. But I knew that by Somebodies she meant the rich men and their wives who lived in the estates, owned cars and worked for the government or big businesses. Their children wore socks and Achimota sandals to school and tied ribbons in their braided hair. The reason we went to school was to turn into Somebody. Sometimes I thought the reason we went to church was the hope that, with God's help, we would become Somebody.

Maa sat with her stained hands folded in her lap, her bare feet on the worn linoleum. Suddenly she looked tired, and the creases on her forehead became more obvious. I wondered how old she was. It struck me that unless she'd had her children late she was probably only as old as Auntie Ruby. Life had worn my mother out.

Maa caught me staring and smiled. I knew then that she had already accepted Auntie Ruby's suggestion. I felt the sting of tears in my eyes, and I looked away.

What could I do? In a matter of weeks, I had run out of choices and all that was expected now was my obedience.

"Auntie Ruby, if it is okay with Maa and Daa, I'll go with you to meet your cousin," I said.

Suddenly, with a loud ripping sound, the rain let itself loose upon our house. I rushed through our small home shutting windows and placing containers here and there to catch the drippings from our rusted aluminum roof. It was easy to spot the leaking places from the brown edges of the watermarks on the ceiling.

Maa chose the same moment to begin a series of breath-stopping coughs. Loud, hacking and frightening. Auntie Ruby was on her feet but didn't know what to do.

"Breathe, Akua. Breathe." Daa stepped into the living room, and his instructions seemed to help Maa as she took in strange-sounding gurgling breaths.

"Gloria, fetch Maa's medicine," Daa instructed. I dashed into their bedroom and brought one of Maa's bottles of bark bitters. Daa opened it and filled the bottle cap. Maa was wheezing.

"Gloria, fetch the ginger paste," she managed between breaths. She had me mix some ginger with a cap full of bitters. She drank it. Then she breathed slowly and deliberately, settling her hurting lungs.

"Ei, Akua," said Auntie Ruby at last. "You have to see a doctor. Maybe Christy can help."

"Christy?" Daa repeated. Auntie Ruby told Daa all about my soon-to-be employer. Just like that, without even trying, she won my father over with the thought of free medical care.

Nothing could save me now.

Half an hour later the rain stopped. Auntie Ruby chartered a drop-in all the way to Labone Estates and paid a lot of money. In my family we never took drop-in taxis. We would make several changes between tro-tro and buses to get wherever we needed to go.

The taxi stopped at the gates of a large house. It was one of the modern square types with a large upstairs balcony.

"This is my uncle's house," said Auntie Ruby proudly. At least her uncle was Somebody.

We let ourselves through the gate to the sound of a dog barking loudly in the back.

"Don't worry, he's chained," said Auntie Ruby.

I hoped so. That deep throaty bark would not come from a regular scrappy Accra mongrel. It had to be a big guard dog, the kind that was fed only meat and marrow.

Large flower pots boasting red and yellow roses hugged the sides of the paved walkway that led off the main driveway.

We rang the bell and someone came to let us in through sliding glass doors. Inside, a welcome breeze met us from a hidden air-conditioner. A young woman opened the door and gave Auntie Ruby a hug. Then she turned and shook my hand.

"You must be Gloria," she said. "I am Christine Ossei."

"She's Dr. Christine Ossei," said Auntie Ruby, as

though she was correcting her. Not everyone had a doctor cousin.

She looked too young to be a doctor. She could have
been one of Effie's mates at catering school.

But she wasn't. She was a doctor and a mother, an
adult.

We sat down and Auntie Ruby began to talk about me
and my parents. She said we were like her family. She said
she had carried me on her own back as an infant and that
I was always very well behaved and obedient.

Her praises were endless. She even said I was smart.

My eyes wandered around the room — the plush green
carpet, the beautiful olive leather furniture, the glass
curio displaying fine glassware, soft music playing from a
stacked sound system.

A houseboy brought in some drinks and cake. I
watched his hands as he flicked the tops off the bottles
with a bottle opener. Auntie Ruby drank her beer from a
glass, but I took my Fanta from the bottle through a
drinking straw. I munched on a generous piece of cake.

Then Dr. Christy said, "Gloria, what are your plans
for your future?"

"I want to sew."

"That's all she ever talks about," said Auntie Ruby, her
famous laugh washing all over us.

"That shouldn't be hard to do in Kumasi. There are
many fine dressmakers there," Dr. Christy said.

"Kumasi?"

"You know I live in Kumasi, don't you?" It was her

turn to be surprised as she turned toward Auntie Ruby.

Auntie Ruby had forgotten to tell me. Kumasi was five hours away by bus. It scared me that I might not be able to see my family for long stretches of time.

Dr. Christy was watching me.

"Don't worry. I come to Accra often to see my family," she said. "I would bring you along, too."

The baby came in holding a bottle of milk.

"This is Sam, my son. He's one and a half," Dr. Christy said. "If you decide to stay with us he will be your charge while I'm at work. I just need someone I can trust to look after him till he can go to nursery school in about two years. Then you could go to sewing school."

"In just two years," said Auntie Ruby, smiling at me. "See, Glo, it couldn't be easier than this. Only one small baby to look after, and Kumasi is nicer than Accra in every way."

It seemed so easy to me, sitting in a beautiful room, eating cake and drinking Fanta. No more selling oranges in the afternoons. No more studying math and English and failing exams. No more homework or punishment from teachers.

Best of all there would be no more questions about the future. Everything was as simple as Dr. Christy had said.

I listened to Dr. Christy's voice rise and fall softly. I couldn't imagine her yelling at me.

I picked up the boy, Sam. He didn't struggle.

"Milk," he said, offering me his bottle.

"He likes you," said Auntie Ruby, beaming.

I laughed. Sam laughed, too. I felt as though I had passed a test. I put Sam on my lap. He smelled sweet, like Johnson's baby powder. Everything smelled sweet in this house, and I ate three large pieces of cake. Nobody said gyae!

By the time the taxi dropped us back home, my mind was made up.

•

A week went by, and the day of my departure came. This time Effie made the fire and cooked the koko. We even had Ideal milk, condensed and evaporated, with the sweetened corn porridge. Daa bought fresh tea-bread from the bread seller, and Maa did not complain when we plastered our slices thickly with Blue Band margarine.

We ate in the living room, our spoons scraping the bottoms of pink plastic cereal bowls.

Afterwards Daa gathered us into prayer, committing my life and my future to God with many supplications.

All that was left now was the parting.

"If she doesn't treat you well, come back home," said Effie. "Run away."

She was sitting on the green loveseat next to me. She was the one person who had asked question after question. What is she like? Does she shadda in designer wear? Is she pretty?

Effie was the only one who had grumbled and said,

"Only the poor give away their daughters like this." Everyone else thanked God for this miracle.

"Nonsense," said Daa. "Dr. Christy is an answer to prayer. She's a good woman and she will treat you well. I pray you behave while you're with her."

"Yes, Daa."

"Remember this is also about your future," Maa said. "Dr. Christy has assured us that she will do her best to establish you as a seamstress. And I feel that there are many other things you will learn from her. How to be a lady, for instance."

"No boy-matter. Understand?" Daa added sternly. "Remember, a boy is never a friend to a girl. Never!"

Effie giggled.

I turned around and tried to silence her with a look.

I worried about Effie because of her boyfriend. I worried that I had accepted her bribes of kelewele, giving the impression to our parents that we'd been together with friends, when she had gone off on her own. All I knew of her boyfriend was that he was a seaman from Tema, the neighboring port city. I didn't even know his name.

"I hope you didn't fill your bag with junk," Maa said. She was looking quite well since she'd started taking some pills that Dr. Christy had sent. Thank God for Dr. Christy.

"Write," said Effie.

Had she forgotten that I didn't like to read or write? I stood up. Effie stood up, too, and we hugged.

"I'll see you soon. Dr. Christy comes to Accra every month," I said.

She nodded. Her eyes filled suddenly with tears.

Through the open window, we saw Auntie Ruby arrive in a taxi. I checked my face for the last time in Effie's mirror. I was wearing my favorite yellow dress, silver stud earrings and a silver necklace. My legs shone with shea butter. My face was powdered lightly, and beads of sweat were forming on the ridge of my nose. I wore my white strappy sandals, which I usually saved for church on Sunday, and all my good possessions were packed neatly in my bag.

"Bye, Daa, bye, Maa. Bye, Effie," I said, looking away from the loss in their eyes. I put my bag in the trunk of the car and shut it with a bang.

One of Adama's children twisted the tap of our communal standing pipe. It gurgled and water gushed out, spilling over the concrete stand.

"Water!" he shouted.

"This means good luck," said Adama.

"Bye, everyone," I said. Then I sat in the back of the taxi next to Auntie Ruby and off we went, blowing dust behind us.

• FOUR •

I first met Bea near the doctors' flats at the Komfo Anokye Teaching Hospital. We lived in one of the three-story doctors' flats, and she lived in the adjacent compound where the nurses' houses stood like matchboxes in a rectangle. The dividing milk-bush hedge separated the doctors from the nurses.

On the far side of the doctors' flats, the bushes grew wild around a variety of trees. Once upon a time all of Kumasi had been nothing but forest. I could imagine what manner of snakes and scorpions might live there still, undiscovered in the undergrowth. Only the street-boys followed their footballs into the bush.

Around the flats, life was carefree. Water flowed in the water pipes and fed the taps in every apartment. The doctors were always chatting and eating at each other's homes, their laughter bouncing off the rough cement-sprayed walls. They didn't seem to care about money. Thick wads appeared out of their pockets and wallets for every favor and purchase.

I remembered my days selling in Accra. It would have

been so much easier selling here at the doctors' flats. They didn't even care that dirty street-boys ate all the mangoes off their trees.

Christine was away on duty at the polyclinic. Going to work was tricky because Sam was always alert for his mother leaving home. I would take him out for a walk or to visit another of the doctors. We usually went to see Dr. Mimi, who had cool cartoons on video. We would spend an hour watching Tom chase Jerry, a thing that made Sam gurgle with laughter.

But by that afternoon, Sam was catching on. Tom and Jerry were no longer so funny.

"Mama," Sam said tearfully, pointing at the door. "Mamama."

I had enough money for a drink at the clubhouse.

"Come, Sam. Let's go and buy Sprite. Then we can sit under an umbrella and watch the doctors play tennis."

"Sprite, Sprite," he sang. Sam understood a treat. I wondered if he understood a bribe.

"Sprite, Sprite," I sang back.

Sam was beautiful. Each morning I bathed him, and if it was a particularly hot day I bathed him again in the afternoon. I floated his yellow rubber ducks in the bath-water for him. I put his tape in the tape player and we sang along with the songs.

"Row, row, row your boat, gently down the stream. Merrily, merrily, merrily, merrily, life is but a dream."

Sam couldn't really speak but he could sing, and he loved that song.

I didn't mind washing Sam's diapers or feeding him. I didn't mind cooking or cleaning, and I loved walking with him and watching the tennis at the clubhouse. Whenever we went out, I made sure Sam looked fine.

"So handsome," I would say, just like the lady on the TV advertisement for A1 Spice. That advert gave me hope that some day I could be as fine as the woman who cooked delicious meals for her beautiful family.

"So handsome," Sam would say in return.

I always wore my good yellow dress. Then Sistah Christy would call me Sunshine Girl.

We had to pass the nurses' quarters on our way to the clubhouse. The driveway curved widely around the bushes, and I wondered whether to walk along the road or cut through the bushes where a dusty-red path had forced itself through.

It was Sam who decided on the path, and he pulled me along to where three girls stood.

"Hello," one of the girls said. "I'm Bea. What is your name?"

"Gloria." I was feeling fine in my Sunshine Girl dress and white strappy sandals. Those girls were still wearing their cream and brown school uniforms, with dirty sandals covered in red dust.

Only last month I, too, had been a schoolgirl in Accra, wearing the same shabby cream and brown uniform.

Bea had very short hair, tightly curled and crawling on her scalp. Her eyes slanted upward, giving her a mischievous look. Her soft full lips hid a very determined jaw. I was only slightly taller than her, and I thought she might be fifteen years old.

"What's the baby's name?" Bea asked.

"Sam."

"Where do you live?"

"D4, with my sister, Dr. Christine Ossei." Auntie Ruby had suggested that I call Christine Sistah Christy instead of Dr. Christy. "She's like your big sister," Auntie Ruby had said.

"That's your sister with the silver Toyota Corolla?" Bea asked. "I like that car."

"Yes." Christine had a really nice car. It was silver and shiny, without a dent or a scratch, and she was proud of it. It was fully air-conditioned.

It felt good to be associated with nice things. My daa, the great chauffeur, had never owned a car. We had never even owned a TV — only the small wireless radio that stood on our windowsill.

"I want you to be my friend," Bea said.

"Okay," I replied coolly. I wondered what her friends were thinking. "We have to go now. I'm taking Sam to the clubhouse to buy Sprite."

"Can I come, too?" Bea asked.

I didn't know what to say.

"Serwaa, Cynthia, later," Bea said. To my surprise she abandoned her friends right there and followed us.

At the clubhouse, I bought a bottle of Sprite for Sam and me. Bea did not order anything so I asked for three glasses. We sat out by the tennis court and shared our first drink, and Bea became my friend.

•

Christine called me Singing Glo because I was always singing. Sam changed the name to Go-go because it was the best he could do. And the rest of our world called me Glo or Glo-glo.

D4 was a two-bedroom flat on the second floor of a three-story block. Christine and Sam slept in one room and I slept in the other, except when Christine was on night duty. Then I slept in her room with Sam. Our two best possessions were a TV and a CD/radio player. In Christine's bedroom there was a radio that doubled as an alarm clock. Up in our apartment we could not hear cockerels crowing at dawn.

Sam also had a destruction-proof Fisher-Price tape player, so all day I could listen to my favorite highlife singers unless Sam demanded his tape music — "Hoki-poki-poki" and "Row, row, row your boat." When Christine came home, she played American pop music and R and B. I liked the Spice Girls.

The living-room wall held pictures of people dear to Christine. There was a picture of Sam's dad, as well as pictures of Sam, Christine and Christine's parents. Each morning Sam demanded to be held up to the picture of his dad, and he would point to it and say Dada. He was a doctor, too. Christine called him JB, and he was studying in England. He called often to speak to Christine and Sam.

Sam was always mystified by the voice coming through the phone. Although he clamored for the phone, he never said a word into it in spite of all the encouragement we gave him.

I took to practicing phone manners with Sam on his toy telephone.

"Hello, Sam?"

"Ha-yo Sam?"

"How are you?"

"Ha ya you?"

I loved TV. In the evenings I watched video upon video of highlife stars singing of heartbreak and love. Then there were the Nigerian films, stories of witchcraft and women marrying for money and men cheating on their wives.

I lived on stories, music and fashion. TV was more real, with men in fancy cars and fashionable women taking more out of life than their true share.

My daa would have judged them all with one word: licentiousness!

Sam and I were watching the latest music video of the Daughters of Glorious Jesus when Christine's phone rang.

It was JB, Sam's dada.

"Is that Gloria?" JB asked, electricity crackling over his voice.

"Yes, Daddy," I gushed into the phone. My voice returned to me hollow and distant.

"Gloria, you are looking after some very precious people," he said. "Treat them well. If you do a good job, I'll have a surprise for you when I return."

I liked Daddy JB at once. His warm voice and hearty laughter made it so easy to like the man whose handsome photo was framed on our living-room wall. Christine called it her wall of fame. She had many more pictures in photo albums and on her dresser.

In my bag was the only photo I owned: Effie and me at the gates of our church, one Christmas when I was about ten.

One day, I thought, I would have albums and picture frames full of my photos to look at and enjoy.

At first I thought about Effie every day. But Bea came by often after school. She would greet Christine with a curtsy and that good-girl voice that we kept for our teachers. Sometimes we went for walks with Sam.

Life had become so much simpler and easier with Christine, and I felt very lucky. It was like having an older sister for a mother — all the care without the bossiness. I ate better than I could ever remember. Sometimes we ate cake for no reason other than dessert.

Effie would have loved it!

• FIVE •

On Saturday we woke up bright and early, long before the full strength of the sun beat hard on us and caused us to perspire.

"Don't bother to shower. The market stinks anyway," said Christine. "I will drop you off to buy the foodstuffs and vegetables while I shop in town for provisions."

Christine was right about the market. They all smelled the same. The odors of smoked and fresh food mingled with the strong smells of decomposing vegetables and not-so-fresh meat and fish.

I didn't bathe, but I took a little time over my face and my hair. I used some face powder and, for the first time, a black pencil on my eyelids.

Not bad, I thought.

"Who will take care of Sam?" I asked Christine.

"Don't worry. I'll take him with me. Kumasi town is small. I'll just push him around in his stroller."

Sam loved his stroller. He didn't get to sit in it often because Christine said strollers were made to be used on smooth sidewalks and in Kumasi there were none.

Pedestrians stole what walking space they could from the dusty sides of the narrow tarred roads. When Sam sat in his stroller, he felt like a king.

Christine had said from the beginning that she did not like the Kejetia Market. She hated the mud, the smell of rotten vegetables, the clogged drains and the dense crowds that squeezed and pushed their way through the narrow alleys. So I alone did all the shopping at the market, week by week. She went shopping only once a month when she bought provisions — sugar, tinned milk, UHT milk and other supplies.

I didn't mind the market. In Accra I had often gone to Mallam Atta Market where Maa traded, only one tro-tro ride away from our home. Here in Kumasi I could browse through merchandise, especially the clothes, and then take a taxi home. Christine let me ride taxis once my basket was full.

Just by the main road we saw Bea with a basket in hand, walking toward the bus stop. Christine stopped for Bea, who ran to the car.

"Are you going to the market?" Christine asked.

"Yes, please. I'm so lucky you saw me," she said, panting.

"And Glo will be happy to have you for company."

Traffic was thick around the Kejetia Circle, and Christine concentrated hard.

"The drivers here have no sense of traffic rules." She shook her head and laughed. "Kumasi can be such a lawless place. But I love it."

Bea leaned forward. "Auntie, that's exactly what my dad says, too. My dad is Dr. Kotoh of obs and gynae."

"Your dad is Dr. Kotoh?" Christine seemed surprised. "I thought you lived at the senior nurses' complex."

"Yes. I live with my mother, Sister Janet of C1. My dad is married to a German woman."

I didn't know Bea's dad was a doctor. I thought doctors were rich, and Bea was not. Suddenly I felt irritated that she was calling Christine Auntie. She had always called her Dr. Christy.

"Auntie, one day I'll be a doctor like you," she said.

"Good for you," said Christine. "I'm afraid that means a lot of study, though. You'll have to work hard and stop gallivanting like you do around the flats."

"I know," she said confidently. "But it's in my blood,"

"I guess it is," Christine said. They both laughed.

Christine wouldn't simply let us out on the street like the taxi drivers did. She wove her way carefully to the side of the road and stopped to let us out some distance away from the market entrance.

"Bye, Sam," I said, waving hard.

"Go-go," shouted Sam, reaching for me. But the car was already weaving back into the traffic.

Bea reached for my hand and laced her fingers through mine.

"Glo, listen. Once we buy our foodstuffs we'll have to go straight home. Our baskets will be too heavy to wander around with. Let's look around first before we shop."

"Where?" I asked. I was still a little irritated with her.

"I'll show you the Jeans-Jeans store. You should see the shadda styles they sell there."

It was as if my eyes were opened for the first time as we began to wander in and out of expensive shops. Madam Cee's fabric store was packed from head to foot with bundles of fabric of all colors. The large woman sat behind an impressive table with the most awful scowl on her face. Her massive arms were crossed on the table where a meter ruler lay. She looked like she would use that ruler on anyone who provoked her.

"Come on, let's go in," whispered Bea.

I hesitated. I knew that kind of woman, face bleached red with deep pencil marks for eyebrows and blood-red lipstick and the look of absolute disdain for those of us who obviously did not have money to spend in her shop.

"I want to show you the latest linen," said Bea.

How could she be so bold? I followed timidly behind.

Madam Cee's eyes followed us around the store. Bea ignored them as she led me around. But even Bea hesitated to run her fingers over the rolls and layers of fabric lining the shelves. I wanted to feel the smoothness of the velvet and the weightlessness of the see-through chiffon they used for wedding veils.

A young girl who worked in the shop approached us.

"Are you buying something?"

"No, I'm just looking," said Bea defiantly.

I tugged at her hand. "Let's go now."

Outside I felt as if I had escaped with my life.

"Could you hear those rolls of material calling, Buy me, wrap me around yourselves and be gorgeous?" said Bea.

"In your dreams," I scoffed. "Let's go and buy our foodstuffs now."

"No. Let's go to the Jeans-Jeans shop. You should see the shoes they have, all from Italy. Italian shoes are the best, I swear," she said, wagging a finger in the air.

I wondered how she would know that, but I was fast realizing that there was much more to Bea than I knew. So we walked down the road hand in hand, carrying our baskets in our free hands. Soon we were at the Jeans-Jeans shop, and it was full of people. There were T-shirts with slogans painted across them in fiery reds and brilliant blues. There were dress shirts and blouses, pants, jeans and corduroys in every color.

An assistant was talking to a client.

"These are designer clothes. Read the labels. Calvin Klein, Yves Saint Laurent, Armani, Versace. That's the reason the prices are what they are," he said.

"Haven't you heard the Chinese are making replicas and merchandisers import them to make even more profit?" said the young woman. "You buy it, then two weeks later the fabric frays." She was sharply dressed in a white three-quarter sleeve shirt and the deepest blue jeans. She held her hair straight back in the severest ponytail. Bea and I watched her.

"Not these clothes," said the assistant. "It's the real thing, straight from America and Europe."

The woman looked like a model in one of the glossy

American magazines. She pushed her large dark glasses onto her head. Her perfume saturated the air.

I couldn't believe my eyes. It was Jemali in person, the jazz-highlife singer! This was where she shopped.

I feasted my eyes on her. Now I knew how I wanted to look when I grew up.

We trailed around the store, touched the things she'd touched, tried the shoes she'd tried. The shop was a shoe heaven, with shoes of all colors sitting on shelves from the ceiling to the floor.

"I like those pointy snakeskin browns with the matching bag," said Bea. She read the designer name. "Gianni."

I preferred the pointed black shoes with a strap across the heel. They reminded me of something Christine would wear.

I felt the buckles on the belts where they hung on a rotating stand. Black leather belts for men, chain belts and the wide elastic belts with their large metal clasps that women wore high on their waists to make their busts look full. There were also glass cases full of bangles and watches with all manner of stones and glittering things.

I stared and stared. Everywhere there were shop attendants watching closely.

I wanted everything.

"When I have some money, I'll come here to buy my clothes," Bea said longingly.

"Me, too."

"The things are beautiful, yes?" It was a heavily accented voice. The speaker was Lebanese.

"Yes," I said.

"You like?"

"Yes, I like."

He picked up a skinny pair of jeans.

"This one will fit. It has spandex. It will stretch. My name is Faisal. I own the store. What's your name?"

"Gloria." I couldn't believe a young man like that could own such a store. I gaped at him.

"You be my friend. You can pay small-small, anything you buy," he said. He was dashing. His dark silky hair spilled over his forehead, but I thought his nose was hawkish and big for his face.

"What about me?" asked Bea.

"Okay, because you are her friend," Faisal said with a shrug.

I laughed. Bea rolled her eyes.

We had spent longer than I thought, and I needed to get home early. I had promised to make palm nut soup for Christine and her friends — Mimi, Julie and Dr. Joe. Dr. Joe had promised to bring his girlfriend, Doyoe, and she was always nice to me.

We returned to Kejetia Market as fast as we could. All of sudden I was attracted to every vendor selling accessories or underpants or even handkerchiefs. Bea laughed at me.

"I thought you were the one from the big city," she said. "You are behaving like a villager come to town."

I bought plantains, onions and tomatoes. I didn't bother to haggle over pennies as I had learned from my mother. In Kumasi, the doctors were too wealthy for

that. I had never seen Christine haggle. I bought kontomire leaves and pepper. Then I bought beef and goat
meat. I bought koobi fish as well. I waited while Bea
bought snails and crabs. I couldn't stand snails.

Our baskets were too heavy to carry by hand so I carried mine on my head. Bea struggled to hold on to hers
but she would not carry the basket on her head.

"Let's take a drop-in taxi," she said at last. "We could
share the cost."

We were turning into our compound when Bea told
the taxi driver to stop.

"Why?" I asked.

"Do you want Christine to see you in a taxi?"

"She doesn't mind if I ride in a taxi."

"You're lucky. My mother will go crazy if she sees me
spending her money on taxis." We paid the taxi driver
and got out. This time I didn't put my basket on my head.

"It was nice today, wasn't it?" Bea asked.

"Yes."

"We should save for those clothes and shoes."

I nodded. "Maybe we could meet later at the clubhouse," I said.

"Sure," said Bea, and she raised her free hand for a
high-five. "First we shower, then we shadda, then we can
sit like ladies and have a drink."

It was nice to have something to look forward to, and
at the edge of the milk bush we parted ways until sunset,
when we could change and for a while become like
Somebodies.

• SIX •

Schools closed for the long vacation and then the rain came. It was hot and humid. I wasn't sure which was worse — noontime in Accra or two o'clock in Kumasi. We could have roasted plantains just by sitting them out in the sun.

In the bedroom, Christine and Sam were putting puzzles together, and the ceiling fan was going at top speed. Christine called them jigsaw puzzles and Sam had about ten of them, which we assembled piece by piece, making beautiful pictures. His favorite was a big red train with a smiley face. He called it Thomas. There were Thomas books, Thomas puzzles and Thomas trains, too. Sam even had a Thomas shirt.

Bea came by one afternoon. She was all excited.

"My friends are outside waiting to meet you," she said. "Maybe we could all walk to town to watch a Chinese film."

"I don't know," I said. Daa never liked me going out that way.

"Go on. Go and ask Dr. Christine," Bea urged.

So I went to knock on Christine's door.

"Sistah Christy, can I go and watch a film with Bea and her friends?"

Christine was building a Lego wall with Sam. She kept on pressing brick onto brick. I waited, holding my breath.

"Okay," she said at last. "Be home by six o'clock."

"Thank you, Sistah." I could not believe my luck.

Bea's friends were standing at the Block D carport. I knew Serwaa and Cynthia, but it was the first time I was meeting Simon. He was tall and skinny and he had an open honest face and a wide grin. He seemed nice.

Bea said Simon was a good guitarist. Soon we were talking about our favorite artists. My first love was Daddy Lumba, of course.

We cut through the medical students' hostel, using the path behind the hospital into town.

"In our band, we're looking for a different groove," Simon said. "We want to adapt hip-hop to highlife."

"Do you really have a band?" I asked.

"Yes."

"I sing."

"We need a singer," said Simon. "Can you join us?"

"But you haven't even heard her," said Bea.

"I can tell by her speaking voice."

"I think you like her," Bea teased. "Tell the truth, Simon." The girls burst out laughing and I couldn't look at Simon. I knew it would get worse if I protested. Those years in school had taught me that.

"Yes, I like her," said Simon, surprising me.

And Bea and Serwaa shouted, "Aieiii!"

•

We began to meet regularly at the Block F carport near the end of the doctors' compound, just where the dust gave way to the mango trees and bushes. Simon brought Jima and Osi to join us. Jima was the drummer and Osi was the keyboardist of the band, which as yet did not have a name. Simon brought along an old guitar but the other two improvised. Jima drummed on every available receptacle, including broken pots, cardboard boxes, wooden crates and old barrels. He was really good and I loved his sounds. There was nothing much for Osi to do. Mostly he would hum his part.

Whenever Sam came along on Christine's duty days, we passed him around from person to person. Someone always had to entertain Sam because otherwise he would get himself very dirty, and there were too many things to put in his mouth.

Simon paid attention to me because he said hip-life depended more on beat and voice. We began to experiment with the songs we knew well. Sometimes Simon would break into rapping in English or Twi. It was so much fun.

Osi came up with a plan. If we joined the youth music ministry of his church, we would have access to the church's instruments on some weekdays.

Christine was willing to let me attend those youth meetings once a week on Thursdays as long as she was home to look after Sam.

"It's a good place to meet people of your age group and still have some supervision," she said.

"We have good Bible studies and discussions," I said, playing up the godly bit. "It's very much like my youth group at home."

"I know there is also prayer time," she smiled. "But none of these have prevented precocious teens from trying things they shouldn't."

"Sistah, I'm not like that."

"No one is like that. Things just happen, hm? Listen, Glo. I know life is very interesting at sixteen and boys may be saying things to you, making suggestions. But it is a smart girl who makes up her mind early who she is going to be and what it takes to be that person. Otherwise you may as well sleep with the night watchmen who spread their mats on verandas, with a million mosquitoes buzzing about their ears."

She was looking at me intently. I opened my mouth to say something but no words came.

"Abroad, they give girls like you condoms to carry in their purses against pregnancy and AIDS. This is Ghana. We don't do such things. Your condom is your mind. Use it when your boyfriends are making suggestions," she said.

"Yes, Sistah."

I thought about what Christine had said. I had heard

it before in religious language from my father and the preachers in church. Everyone seemed to think sex was all we teenagers thought about.

On Saturday, Christine's department doctors had a party. Christine and her friends had their hair done at Yramesor Salon. Yramesor was Rosemary turned the other way. It was the best salon in town. I watched them transform before my eyes in Christine's bedroom, giggling like Effie and her friends, trying out lipstick and eyeliner and glitter, changing bags and trading shoes. Often Sam got in the way so I wrap-tied him on my back to keep him from trouble. I ran errands to and from Julie's apartment, fetching shoes and bags and tissues. Then at three o'clock they left in Christine's car for the party at the Georgia Hotel.

I wanted to visit the clubhouse, and I knew Bea would love that, too, so I changed Sam's shirt and off we went, cutting through the milk-bush hedge to the nurses' compound.

Bea's mom, Sister Janet, was a large woman who kept her straightened hair in a thinning ponytail. Her eyes were small and without humor.

"Bea, your friend is here," she said. Then she turned away without greeting me. "Make sure you finish the dishes before you go wandering." Her voice was scratchy, as though she'd lost it a while ago and found only a part of it again.

"Yes, Mama," Bea replied from inside.

Bea came through the kitchen door and gave me a

mischievous wink, but I had on my good-girl face and I didn't wink back. Sam held on tightly.

"Mama, can I bring Gloria to the kitchen?"

"Yes." Sister Janet's answer was short.

I followed Bea to the kitchen and stood by the door while she washed dishes in murky soapy water, then rinsed them in an aluminum pan of clear water. The kitchen was hardly bigger than a cupboard, and most of their cooking was actually done out in the yard where the coal pot stood among other soot-stained pots and pans.

In some ways I was reminded of my home in Accra. I guess it was just that look of weariness, even among the pots and pans.

I didn't volunteer my help. I was bathed and well dressed for the afternoon, and besides, I had Sam. So I talked to her from the doorway.

"Where do you want to go?" Bea asked, transferring plates with dripping hands.

"To the clubhouse."

"Do you have money?"

"Just enough for a drink," I replied. "Do you have money?"

"No."

Soon the dishes were all arranged on the draining board. Bea wiped the area around the sink and mopped the floor. Then she washed her hands and dried them on the front of her dress.

"Wait for me in the living room while I change," she said.

I was glad she was going to change.

"Use deodorant," I said.

The small living-dining was next to the kitchen. I looked around at the old dusty armchairs huddled in the gloom. Heavy gabardine curtains drooped on sagging wire supports above the window, blotting out the sunlight.

There were several photographs on the room divider. I was looking at them when Bea returned in a clean blue-and-white dress with a white collar and short sleeves.

"That's my father," she said proudly, pointing to a distinguished-looking man in a group photo. "Dr. Kotoh."

Her mother was in the photograph, too. She looked much younger and slimmer.

"Your father's handsome," I said. "Does he work on ward C1 with your mother?"

"No, he's an obstetrician-gynecologist," she replied. "He works in the A Block."

"What's an obsti — whatever you said?"

"A woman's doctor, dealing with pregnancy and such," she replied. "He does operations, too."

I thought of her doctor father and her nursing-sister mother. Bea should have been one of those "daddy's children" who went to private schools and wore ribbons in their hair. My old school in Accra had people like Bea whose fathers were Somebodies, rich and important. But the children of ex-wives, concubines and second wives were often left to struggle in poverty with their mothers.

The clubhouse on Saturday afternoon was buzzing

with life. There were tennis-playing men in their whites, beer bellies pushing against their tight shorts. From time to time they mopped away at the sweat with towels their ball boys handed them. Others sat on white deck chairs, their towels hanging around their necks. The bar boys served Star and ABC beer in tall glasses, saying, "Yes, sah. T'ank you, sah!"

I noticed five young women about Effie's age sitting with a group of men sipping beer and soft drinks. They were all fashionably dressed and made up, too.

"Let's sit here," said Bea, pointing at some chairs near the entrance to the courts. Sam sat on my lap. We sipped our drinks and watched the game, and the group to our right got larger and larger.

Someone tapped me on my shoulder. It was Dr. Joe.

"Gloria, how are you? Hey, Sam!"

He held his arms open for Sam. Sam climbed over to him.

"Where's Christine?" he asked.

"She's gone to the party at Georgia Hotel."

There was someone behind Dr. Joe. She was a very pretty girl but she was not Doyoe.

"Hello," said the girl. Her smile was friendly.

"I'll keep Sam for a while," said Dr. Joe. I followed them with my eyes to the other group.

"All the girls are from the nurses' training college," Bea said. "I've seen most of them."

Sam looked happy as he sat on Dr. Joe's friend's lap.

"I wonder if Doyoe knows Dr. Joe's friend?" I said.

"I bet she's his other girlfriend," Bea chuckled. "All the doctors have nurse girlfriends."

But I didn't think Dr. Joe would have a second girl-friend.

We turned our attention to the game. More people came in. Some of them were older than Dr. Joe's lot.

"Those are my father's friends," Bea whispered.

They didn't recognize Bea. The place was full. There were no more deck chairs for the people coming in. Soon we'd have to go.

I heard Sam's cry. He was tired of listening to strangers. I went over to get him.

"Small girl, what's your name?" one of the men in Dr. Joe's company asked.

"Aah, you, too," said Dr. Joe. "*Ogyam*, this one is too young! Christine will kill you if you go that way."

Everyone burst out laughing.

"I fear that Christine," said the man who'd asked my name. "Don't tell her I asked your name, hm?"

I laughed, too. I knew they were joking.

"Say bye," I said to Sam, but Sam turned away. And the stranger's eyes watched us all the way to the gate.

• SEVEN •

The magazine was called *Brides*, and it lay on Bea's mother's table with other papers. It was at least ten years old but it still had its cover on. Someone had scribbled with a blue pen all over it. Bea said it belonged to her mother's friend.

I leafed through the magazine, staring at the pretty young women dressed in white. Most of the models were white, too. When we found a black woman, we studied her from head to toe.

Bea could speak of nothing except her confirmation at the end of the year. She was going to dress up all in white, just like a bride, she said.

"Have you been confirmed?" she asked.

"In our church we get baptized in water. I'll have to wait until I'm married to wear white."

We looked through the pages and dreamed. I picked one dress. It had a wide skirt and no sleeves. She picked another. It was figure hugging and long.

"When are you going to have your dress made?" I asked.

"Soon." She turned the pages. "The other day I saw white shoes that looked almost like these at the Jeans-Jeans shop, and they fit me exactly."

"They would cost a lot of money."

"I'll ask my dad to buy them for me." She turned the pages of the magazine slowly.

"Listen to this," I said. "Yesterday when Sistah Christy entered the flat, she was barefooted."

"Why?" Bea asked.

"Someone vomited on her shoes in the ward. So when she got to the complex, she took off her shoes and threw them in the garbage. And it was a really nice pair, too!"

"I would have fetched them and washed them," Bea said.

"I wanted to but Sistah Christy said she didn't want those shoes in her house."

"It's nice to be rich," said Bea. "I have never heard of anyone throwing away a good pair of shoes."

"Me neither."

"How much does Christine pay you?" Bea asked abruptly.

"Pay me? She's my sister. She doesn't pay me."

"So she doesn't even pay you a little bit for all the work you do?"

"She's my sister," I said again. Bea was beginning to annoy me.

My daa had declined pay from Christine, asking instead that she take me as a sister, treat me well and help me acquire a vocation. Sisters were forever, much better than pay, my daa had said.

"Don't you want those jeans from Jeans-Jeans?" Bea asked. "The ones with zippers across the pockets and along the sides? And I want that red T-shirt with Diva written across it in sparkling silver."

I wanted a lot of things, but I was used to not having most of the things I wished for. I was not like Effie. She had complained much about Daa's unemployment and now she had a boyfriend. Someone said seamen traveled far and always brought good gifts. Perhaps Effie was getting some of the things she wanted.

"Gloria, everyone buys things on credit. Remember Faisal, the guy who likes you? He'll let us buy on credit."

Bea amazed me. She never had money. Not even for Fanta or Sprite when we went to the clubhouse. How would she pay for those expensive clothes at Jeans-Jeans?

•

On Wednesday, Christine brought home a letter for me. The envelope was a fancy pink one with red roses at one corner.

"I think it may be from your father. If you write to him, I'll post the letter for you when I go to town on Friday," Christine said.

I recognized Effie's script, loose and confident in blue ink. I thought of asking Christine to read the letter to me but I held my tongue. What if there was a secret in the letter? I wondered if I could ask Simon to read it to me.

Simon was seventeen and in his second year of SSS.

He was good at math but he was in love with music. In just a year from September he would be entering KNUST to study engineering. But in the meantime he dreamed only of music.

I wished he was going to study medicine. I wanted to marry a doctor. Perhaps I could change his mind. Medicine was far better than engineering.

Deep down, I knew I couldn't ask Simon or Christine to read my letter to me. If people knew you couldn't read or write well, they thought you were stupid. I couldn't let anyone think that anymore.

To get to the church we had to take a tro-tro from Bantama Circle to Kejetia and change at the lorry station to take another tro-tro to Asafo. Three Thursdays out of four, I was able to make this trip with Bea, Simon, Jima and Osi. On the last Thursday of every month, Sistah Christy had a special evening with her team and I had to look after Sam. Bea was Catholic but her mother gave her permission to go anyway. Bea said her mother was fine with her going out so long as she was with me. Lately it felt as if she was living in our flat.

Although youth meeting began at six, we always got there an hour and a half early because Osi had a key. We set up the room and got in an hour's practice.

We were getting better all the time. We had three songs that we performed really well. Out of these, one had a Jesus theme and two were secular.

Simon was the writer. He had pages of lyrics in Twi and English. Because my reading was slow, I always asked him to sing through the songs with me. Jima gave the beat and Simon rapped. I was good at memorizing if I listened well and often enough.

"Do it again," I said.

The third time, I began to rap along with him. The fourth time, Bea got fed up and went for a walk. She didn't like it when she was not the center of everyone's attention. The fifth time, I had learned it all.

"Ei, you're quick," said Simon.

I smiled. Our faces were close together.

"F Block," said Osi suddenly.

"What?" asked Simon.

"F Block, that's the name of our band," said Osi. And just like that we had a name.

"F Block, let's try 'Push It' again," said Simon like a radio announcer.

And we did, again and again. Simon strummed a melody on his guitar. I rapped, he rapped. Jima drummed. Osi was a natural at finding parts, and he played the keyboard.

I felt close to Simon. So when his arm crept up on my shoulder, I let it rest there in spite of my father's words, "No boy-matter!"

Life was not as evil as my father made it out to be. In certain places, people enjoyed their freedoms without guilt. Friendship with Simon felt good.

I had made friends with the other boys and girls in the youth group, and those evenings were filled with laughter. After youth group, I asked Simon if he knew where kelewele was sold. He did and we went off by ourselves to buy some. On the way I told him all about Effie.

"One day I'll meet her," he said.

"You'll like her," I said. "She's so fun and adventurous."

"So are you."

And he linked his arm through mine as we wound through the taxis parked near the stadium where the vendors sold every kind of food. There we waited our turn beside the line of small tables where kerosene-wick lamps cast feeble shadows on the ground. We were served Kumasi kelewele in newspaper, but it wasn't as good as my Daavi's kelewele in Accra.

We walked along the street side by side, eating hot spicy kelewele. We could hardly speak as we sucked in the night air to cool our burning hot tongues.

"I know a short cut," said Simon, leading me across a park. Stepping into the darkness, he pulled me close and gave me my first kiss on the lips.

There it was, just as I had seen it on TV. It tasted funny, and I wondered why people did it. Then we walked back to the doctors' flats, a little quieter than before.

•

Dr. Joe came to visit. Christine sent me to the kitchen to make them some tea while Sam played with his chunky blocks of Lego.

Joe was dashing, just as I imagined Simon would be

one day. He looked great in his dark blue jeans and sky blue golf shirt. He had on a new pair of dark glasses, and his charm dripped all over everybody like a bottle of cold beer in the sun. No wonder girls liked him so much. He was a body builder with big arms and the broadest shoulders. Even Simon and Osi admired him in his muscle T-shirts and khaki cut-offs.

Bea, Cynthia and Serwaa agreed he was the finest when he stripped down to his waist while he washed his car on Saturday mornings.

Apart from his looks, he was really nice. Christine was always happy whenever Joe called on us. She said they were best friends and had been study partners in school. But she also said Dr. Joe was bad news for the girls.

"They all fall for him," she said. "Then they come crying to me later when they find it's Doyoe he loves. What can I do? He's such a flirt!"

I waited for the kettle to whistle. Two tea bags were waiting inside two Princess Diana coffee mugs. I remembered that Sam would want some milk, too. At night he preferred his milk in a bottle and we obliged him, although Christine worried that it would rot his teeth.

The water boiled. I made the two teas first. I made Sam's milk and set it in cold water to cool. I put two spoonfuls of sugar in each mug and then Ideal milk from a freshly opened tin. Christine liked a lot of milk in her tea. I remembered she had bought digestive biscuits, so I placed six of them on a saucer for them to share. I took two out for Sam and me.

Just as I took the tray in, Christine exclaimed loudly.

"Oh, no, Joe," she said.

The way she said it raised goosebumps on my skin. It was as though someone had died. I gripped my tray firmly, catching the pained expression on Joe's face. Something was definitely wrong.

"If Doyoe hears this, she'll drop me for sure," Joe said miserably.

"Glo, put the tray down and change Sam," Christine said, turning toward me.

I tried to pick Sam up but he wouldn't hear of it. The harder I tried, the more he screamed.

"Just leave him and go," said Christine. "Tidy the kitchen or something."

I left Sam with his mother and busied myself in the kitchen as they talked.

Someone was in trouble. Dr. Joe stayed for a long time talking softly to Christine. Sam fell asleep on the couch, and when I had made the kitchen spick and span, I went off to bed.

• EIGHT •

Since my very first kiss in the park, I had begun to braid my hair each night. Each morning when my chores were done, I combed out the braids, raising my hair in a small flat-top afro. Bea and the others had started making fun of Simon and me but I didn't care, so long as it didn't spread to Christine's ears.

Friday came around and I had heard enough little bits of conversation to know that Doyoe had broken up with Joe.

Dr. Joe loved jolof, especially when one cooked the sauce with green peppers. So when Christine sent me to the market on Saturday, I was glad she wanted green peppers as well as beef. I decided to cook jolof on Sunday as consolation for Dr. Joe.

Bea and I took the tro-tro from Bantama Circle to Kejetia Market.

"Wait," she said, stopping at the roadside. She passed me her basket, opened her purse and brought out a mirror and black eyeliner. I watched as she carefully outlined her eyelids with black kohl. She passed me the pencil.

Next she took out a thing of purple lipstick and carefully applied it on her lips. With one finger she cleaned the edges just so and stood transformed before my eyes.

"Your turn," she said.

I took my turn with the eyeliner and the lipstick.

"Don't you have eyeshadow?" I asked.

"No," she said. "My ma does not use eyeshadow."

And suddenly we were full of giggles. Then we remembered that we were supposed to be more mature, so we stopped.

"I have a friend whose mother sells shea butter in the market. Let's leave our baskets with her while we walk to the shops," said Bea. We found her friend Doris busy measuring shea butter in cans, and she agreed to keep our baskets at her stall.

Before we knew it, we were at the Jeans-Jeans shop and it was busy. Someone said they had just received a large consignment of clothing. We walked slowly through the shop looking at the bags, the shoes and the clothes. We circled once, then again.

Bea pointed at a pair of shoes.

"That's what I want, and that bag," she said. The white bag matched the shoes, which had a pointy full front and a strap at the back as well as a gold buckle at the side. They were fancy and looked expensive displayed with the bag.

I said nothing. Anyone could want anything. Wanting was just like wishing or dreaming. I had done that all my life.

"My friend!"

The deep throaty voice startled me. I turned to face Faisal. I wondered if he greeted everybody that way.

"Hi," I said.

"Why haven't I seen you in a long time?"

"I've been busy."

"Not too busy for your friends, I hope." His smile was friendly. Even his eyes smiled.

"Hi," said Bea.

"Ah, my friend's friend," he said. "How are you?"

"My name is Bea," she said, looking Faisal squarely in the eyes.

That was the thing about Bea. She wasn't shy. But sometimes her boldness irked me, especially when she wanted all the attention. I wished I was bolder, like her.

"You want to buy some clothes?" he asked.

Bea pointed to the shoes and the bag.

"Those shoes, 500,000 cedis," he said.

"What about the white leather bag?"

"350,000 cedis."

"You said we could pay small-small," said Bea.

"How much can you pay me today."

"Twenty thousand," said Bea.

Faisal asked an attendant to bring him the shoes in Bea's size. Bea tried them on. She strutted about the room.

We followed him to a small back room that served as an office. He pulled out a ledger book and proceeded to find a page. I saw him write in the date.

"Name?"

"Beatrice Kotoh."

Bea was careful to spell her name. Faisal marked a cross on one of the shoeboxes and wrote BK and the date. In his ledger he wrote Beatrice Kotoh in full and included a description of the shoe: Ivory white Pazotti.

"First you buy the shoes, then after you buy the bag, okay?"

Bea nodded.

"But what if you run out of bags?" she asked.

"Don't worry, I have enough bags for you."

Lastly he entered Bea's first instalment of twenty thousand cedis. Then he handed her a receipt.

"Thank you," said Bea. And she folded the receipt away in her pocket.

"And you, my friend, you want to buy something?" he asked, turning to me.

I wanted to say I'll buy those jeans we looked at last time, but I had no deposit.

He opened the drawer of the desk he'd been writing on. He took out a brand-new tube of lipstick and handed it to me.

"This is for you," he said. And his tongue curled over the *r*, drawing it out.

"For me?"

"Take it," he said. But as I reached for his hand, he grabbed hold of mine for just a moment, scraping my palm with his fingernail. I felt the blood rush into my ears.

"Thank you," I said. But I sounded breathless.

"Come and buy the jeans next time," he said. "I'll give you a good price, my friend."

As soon as we stepped into the street, Bea said, "He loves you, Glo. I should have asked you to buy the shoes for me. He would have given you a better price. Next week you have to ask him for a price reduction for me."

It frightened and thrilled me that Faisal seemed to like me in a special way. I looked back at Jeans-Jeans. It was still as busy as ever. Cars had lined up across the street.

How did people find all that money just for clothes, I wondered. Effie and I had felt lucky with selections from Auntie Ruby's Bend-Down Boutique, when she received bales of used clothing from overseas. We called it oburoni-wawu, the belongings of dead white people. Maa said they were not necessarily dead, only tired of their clothes.

Outside in the heat of the morning, we remembered who we really were. We rushed back to the market and filled our baskets with food. I bought the meat, and tomatoes, peppers and onions and a thick wad of kontomire leaves. It was humid and flies buzzed everywhere, disoriented by the heat and the smells.

Christine had asked me to buy extensions for her hair, so I stopped by the large hair kiosk, Black Beauty, to buy three packets of brownish-black hair highlighted with streaks of blond. I wondered if she'd like them. Christine was simple in her taste. I'd only ever seen her use black. I had five thousand cedis of my own money, tips from

Christine and Dr. Julie, so on an impulse I bought a packet of simple black extensions for myself, an eyebrow pencil and brown face powder after a bit of bargaining.

●

I was glad when the doorbell sounded because I was alone for the evening. I had just finished cleaning the kitchen and was wondering what to do.

It was Bea, all bathed and fresh.

"Where is everybody?" she asked as she walked into the living room and found everything tidy and quiet.

"Sistah Christine and Sam have gone to a get-together at the university. She went with Julie and Mimi."

"Oh, I know. It's their graduation class get-together. That's why she took Sam," she said. "They like to show off their husbands, wives and babies. I bet the complex is half empty."

It did seem rather quiet, and outside there were hardly any cars in the carport. Looking out our balcony, I could count on one hand the number of apartments that were lit in E Block and F Block.

"They said they would be away until ten o'clock," I said.

"Probably even later," said Bea. "Let's have a party." Her slanted eyes were wide and bright.

"Are you crazy?"

Bea laughed, and she did sound a little crazy. But she pushed and prodded until I found every last cedi I had and then we were off to buy kelewele.

I followed her along the driveway up to Bantama Circle. For two hundred yards along the roadside, vendors sat on wooden benches behind tables of large steaming aluminum pots of fried meats, stews, rice, kenkey, plantains and yams.

We put our money together and bought a large amount of kelewele and asked the seller to add roasted groundnuts. She wrapped it all up in old newspaper. Minding the busy street, we walked back to the doctors' flats.

I wondered what kind of party we would have with just Bea and me and some kelewele.

"So what next?" I asked.

"You'll see."

Back at the flats, we found Simon and Jima at the carport at F Block, just where the mango tree stood.

"Ei, Bea, see who are here," I said, surprised.

"Bea told us to meet you here," said Simon. "Didn't she tell you? It's her birthday."

"Yes, I'm sixteen today," she said. "And we are going to celebrate."

It felt strange to do things behind Christine's back, but it was clear Bea had it all planned out and I could only hope that we would not be discovered.

We walked quickly up the stairs and I prayed I would not bump into anyone I knew. I unlocked the door and in we went. Bea led everyone to the living room.

I served the kelewele and groundnuts in a dish, took out four glasses and filled them with orange drink.

We sang "Happy Birthday" for Bea and she stood beaming through it all. Then I put on the stereo rather low, because I didn't want anyone telling Christine about loud music from her flat. Bea gave us news from the hospital, and I told them about Dr. Joe and Doyoe's break-up, but Bea had already heard. Bea got all her information from the nurses at the training college. She knew everyone.

Bea and I showed the boys our choreography for "Push It." Simon wanted water so I went to fetch him a bottle from the fridge. When I returned to the living room, Bea was sharing the couch with Jima, and Simon was sitting by himself in the armchair.

"Come here," said Simon. So I went over and sat by him. We watched TV and Simon put his arm around my neck. I could tell that Bea and Jima were kissing, and soon Simon kissed me.

After a while I began to feel uncomfortable. What if Christine opened her door and found us like this? I got up and began to tidy the dishes away.

"Let's dance," said Bea.

"I think you'd better all go before I get into trouble." I was getting worried.

"She's right," said Jima.

"Just one dance," Bea pleaded. "What's a birthday party without dancing?"

So we danced, all four of us, but my heart was not in it. I really wanted everyone out.

At last the song ended. It was nine-thirty. We heard

the sound of a car pulling into the carport. I went to the window to check it out. It wasn't a car I recognized. Thank God.

"Thank you," said Bea happily. "You're a good friend and I have enjoyed my birthday party."

She tried to hug me. I wriggled free of her arms.

"You have to go now," I said. "Christine will be home soon."

It was with much relief that I shut the door behind them. I rushed through the living room cleaning up every trace of their presence. I filled up the water bottle and put the dishes away. I stuffed the kelewele wrappers deep into the rubbish bin. I sprayed air freshener everywhere.

Then my beating heart settled little by little.

• NINE •

Christine liked her new hair extensions. She leaned over the railing and called Julie and Mimi to come up to see them. Dr. Julie said I was avant-garde. She often used terms I had never heard before.

They were talking about hairstyles when the hair braider arrived to do Christine's hair.

Mimi was leaving that afternoon for Accra, so Christine wrote a note for her mother.

I wondered when Christine would plan a trip to Accra for us. Two months had passed since I had come to Kumasi.

I watched as her pen sped on the notepad, spitting out words between commas and periods.

"Grab me an envelope from my desk," she said.

When I returned with the envelope, she said, "Glo, write a note to your family. Mimi will give it to my mother and she'll send it to your house for you. And I could send them some money, too."

The hair braider was setting up, separating the extensions into smaller thicknesses of artificial hair and arranging them on the arm of the couch. Her fingers moved quickly.

I hesitated. Christine handed me the pen and notepad.

"It will take me a little while," I said.

"You have up to an hour while I wait for my ride," said Mimi, taking Christine's letter. "Bring your letter to me at my apartment."

I disappeared into my room. I thought hard and wrote to my sister.

Dear Effie,

Does a friend of Sister come to Accra. I writ quik note to say am well and happy and come home vist soon with Sister Cristy.

Yor sister,

Gloria.

I folded the note carefully and put it in an envelope, sealing it carefully with a bit of spit. On the envelope I wrote, *Miss Effie Bampo.*

"Are you done?" asked Christine.

"Yes, Sistah."

"Hurry up, go and give the note to Mimi and come and watch Sam," she said.

When I got back Sam was riding his yellow car around the living room and along the corridor, blowing his horn and shrieking with laughter. I followed him around for a bit. Then I went to start the cooking.

First I allowed the cubes of beef to simmer in their own juices with pureed onions and salt. Then as the red of the meat juices faded into pink and brown, I added a small amount of vegetable oil. Oil made everything taste better. I crushed ripe red plum tomatoes in Christine's brand new blender. The blender was so much quicker than the grinding stone I used at home. I added the crushed tomatoes to the meat, lowered the heat and sat down to pick the rice clean.

"Gloria, come and split the extensions for Mary, please. She'll go a lot faster with some help," Christine called.

"Sistah, let me just add the rice on to cook."

"What are you cooking?"

"Jolof rice," I answered.

"Aha, Glo, who is coming for dinner?"

"No one," I answered. Suddenly I was too shy to say I had Dr. Joe in mind.

Christine laughed. "Are you sure, Glo?"

Sam shouted, "What, what?"

"What" was his new word, and he always turned his hands up the way some people did whenever they said "Why?" He seemed to be amazed by the turning of his own hand.

I washed the rice and scooped it into the pot to cook in the sauce and grated in some nutmeg.

When I cooked, I felt better about things. I relaxed as I stirred the pot. My confidence grew as I measured salt and spices with my eye and mixed them into my cooking.

And the uneasiness of writing that note to my sister faded gradually.

"Glo, are you done? Come and split the hairs for me, please," Christine shouted once more.

I joined her in the living room and began to split the hairs quickly. Mary's hands wove the extensions deftly into Christine's straightened hair. I watched as she picked Christine's hair at the scalp and wound the extension around them before she parted the hair for braiding. It was an intricate job, but how her hands flew. The finished braids were thin, smooth and very long.

"What did you say to your sister?" asked Christine as the hour passed.

"Oh, I just said we were all doing well."

"That was it?"

"I said I was happy and Sam was a good boy," I lied.

"Didn't you say anything about Bea and your youth meetings and your band?"

Christine took my silence to mean dismay.

"Why, Glo, do you think I don't know about your band? You kids think we're totally blind, eh?" she laughed.

I laughed, too.

"One day your band will have to play for me," she said.

"Yes, Sistah."

"Since you're making jolof, I think I'll call Doyoe for dinner," she said.

"How about Dr. Joe?"

"Not tonight," she said. "Take a note to her for me, please."

I fetched the notepad and pen I'd used earlier.

"Write, 'Dear Doyoe.'"

The pen almost flew out of my hand as I realized that I was going to have to write the note. I froze.

"Dear Doyoe," she repeated, watching me.

I began to sweat on my nose and on my forehead and in my palms. This felt worse than school. I wrote the letter D.

"What's wrong, Glo? Can't you write?"

"I don't spell well," I stammered.

"Never mind then. It can wait until I'm done."

I escaped to the kitchen. The jolof was cooking perfectly but I felt no pride. I felt sick. I sliced cabbage and boiled it. Christine was wary of lettuce and other fresh leaves. I covered the dining table with a cloth and laid the table — one place for Christine at the table head and a place for Doyoe beside her. I set Sam's place by his high chair. This time I set no place for myself. I bustled about with placemats, glasses and forks and knives. I set our white plates in place.

"Your girl is really neat," I heard Mary say.

And Christine said, "Yes, Gloria is a good girl."

I stayed in the kitchen and watched the small flames of the gas fire lick the bottom of the cooking pot.

My secret was out, before Christine and a stranger. There was nothing more said until Mary was done. It had taken two and a half hours to put probably a hundred tiny braids in.

"Glo, bring the pen and notepad to the table," said Christine. She swung Sam about, held him up and kissed him. Sam kissed her back. I stood by the dining table and waited.

"Sit down," said Christine.

She was still playing with Sam, and Sam was pulling at her brand new extensions, trying to pull them out of the ponytail at the back of her head, but she swung him around, avoiding his small hands. I pulled at the chair closest to me, away from the place settings, and sat down.

"Write, Hi Doyoe."

I wrote Hi. She sounded out D-o-y-o-e slowly.

"Listen for the sounds of the consonants and the vowels," she said. She spelled it out for me and I wrote, *Gloria has cooked jolof and you must not say no to our invitation. She is to wait and not return unless you come with her. Love, Christine.*

Slowly, the words were sounded out and spelled. Perspiration dotted my brow and nose. The pen was slippery between my thumb and finger but I wrote on, feeling like a little child.

"Good," said Christine when she had read the note. "Now run along and hand it to her."

Doyoe took twenty minutes to change and make ready for dinner. She was usually very casual but this time when she came out of her room she was dressed up and made up.

She was probably thinking Joe was coming to dinner as well, but I said nothing. I noticed her short jean skirt, her white bareback top and the strappy red sandals on her slender feet.

Doyoe had polished nails. Christine never polished

her nails. She said that she washed her hands about three hundred times a day because of hospital work and had no use for nail polish.

My nails were short. I kept them chewed down, a habit that Christine scolded me about. Perhaps if I painted my nails, I'd take better care of them.

Christine had served the dishes up in her best Pyrex bowls, the rectangular ones with pale flowers etched into the sides. The clear glass lids of her bowls were steamed over from the hot rice and cabbage. Cold water from the fridge was served in a glass jug instead of the usual bottles, and fresh orange juice half filled a pitcher. Christine had set an extra place for me.

At first we ate in silence. Sam scattered his rice over the tablecloth and Christine scolded him. They talked about Christine's ward and Doyoe's ward. They talked about this boss and then another. Doyoe mentioned Dr. Kotoh, Bea's father.

"I don't know what's wrong with him," she complained. "He's asking me the hardest questions all the time and then he tells all the other members in our team that I don't read over my lecture notes, even though I spend all night reading."

Evidently it was very hard to become a doctor.

The beef was soft and spicy just the way I liked it, flavored full of ginger and onions. I munched happily, noisily.

Christine looked up at me. She kept looking and not even blinking.

I shut my mouth over my meat and chewed like a lady. It was tough using a fork, but Christine insisted on a fork for rice, not a spoon. And so I struggled to keep a good mouthful of rice on my fork, filling my mouth two or three times before I had enough to chew on.

I wished I could have written all this for Effie to read. Embarrassment flooded over me as I remembered the note, making my ears and cheeks warm. I sipped on my glass of cold water.

Christine wanted to talk to Doyoe privately, so after supper I cleared the table. Then I dished the rest of the jolof into an enamel bowl. I was going to take it to Dr. Joe.

I called for Sam and patted his bottom. His pull-up diaper was light. Sam was getting the message about messes and potties. Soon he would be ready for preschool. I put on his sandals, fetched the small woven basket and covered the bowl with a dishcloth. I shut the door quietly behind us, and then we moved as sure footed and silent as cats in the night.

Dr. Joe was watching TV with two friends when we arrived at his apartment in F Block. The doctor who had asked my name at the clubhouse was there, and they were arguing loudly about soccer and the African Cup of Nations.

"You again," he said when I greeted them. "You never told me your name."

"Don't tell him," said Joe.

"My name is Gloria," I said. Then I gave Dr. Joe the basket.

"Is Doyoe still with Christine?" Dr. Joe asked, lifting the lid of the enamel dish.

I nodded. So he knew.

"The food smells good. Tell Christine I said thanks," he said.

"Please bring the bowl and the basket back later," I said.

"Gloria?" It was the other man. "Is that your cooking?"

"Yes," I said proudly.

"I can't wait to taste it."

• TEN •

On Monday, Christine came back with books and note-books. She put them on the table and spread them out. *First Aid in English*, *Student's Companion*, Ladybird Readers and *Longman's Writing Exercises for Grade 2*.

"Glo, you're going to learn to read and write. It's not enough that you cook well, or sing or sew or whatever. The difference in life is made by literacy."

I was torn between hope and fear. What was cool about a sixteen-year-old reading grade two books? I could never let Bea or Simon see me with these books. But what if they came by when Christine was teaching me?

"We'll work in the evenings," Christine said, as though she could read my mind. "If you work hard you should make fast progress because I'll be tutoring you one on one. I don't know what they teach in the public schools. It's all about lashes for every tiny infraction and running chores and errands for your teachers, and then they let you pass exams."

That was only half true. Many of my mates had learned to read regardless of errands and lashes. But it was comforting to know Christine didn't blame me. I hoped she wouldn't yell at me for making mistakes. I hoped that this time everything would make sense and I would learn what I hadn't been able to in ten years of education.

So we began the lessons. Reading was more fun with Sam's books and read-along tapes. My finger traced a path beneath the words, and I read after the speaker, within the pauses. In time I knew exactly what she was going to say and how she was going to say it. I began to lift the ends of my sentences, imitating the sing-song British accent as I read, "Not me, said the monkey."

I felt sure I was reading when I recited the whole book without the tape, but Christine said it was all by-heart memorizing. She taught me when she wasn't busy and she gave me homework for when Sam was taking a nap.

I read and read until I could read everything that Peter and Jane did with the red ball in the Ladybird book. I read through 1A, 1B and 1C and right through to book 3C. This time Christine agreed that I was sounding the words and reading. She gave me spelling tests.

"Here's where you learn things by heart," she said. "Sounding does not always do it."

I no longer spent long hours in the evening talking with Bea, although I continued to go to youth meetings and band meetings. I could tell that I was making progress. Even Sam was pretending to read. It tickled Christine to hear him make up sentences while his finger trailed the words in a book.

"You're so smart, Sam," she said.

Simon registered our band for the Anansekrom night at the cultural center. There were several student bands scheduled for the event, and the Prempeh College band, Black Masters, was the most popular. On Thursdays that was all we talked about, especially when the posters appeared in town.

The date was September 3, the end of the long vacation and just before the new school year began.

"Gloria, you've never seen Kumasi like this. Town will be so funky," said Bea.

"Have you asked your sister if you can go?" Simon asked.

When I arrived home, Christine was packing up her stuff to go to bed. She had been working on her files. I summoned my courage.

"Sistah, my band is playing at Anansekrom on September 3," I said. "Can you come? I mean, can I go?"

"Oh, Glo, I was planning our first trip to Accra," she said. "It's months since I brought you down here and I have a few days off at last."

"Oh, no," I gasped. I had to play this first gig with F Block. I couldn't miss that, not even for a trip to Accra.

"I have to go to Accra, Glo, but you can stay and perform with your band. I know how much this means to you."

"Sistah, thank you," I said, hugging her. Daa had been right about Christine. Not many adults would have cared how much this performance meant to me. But she cared.

We practiced hard every day. Simon made me sing and sing and sing. I had to practice my dances, too. Then we had to plan our clothes. It was an easy choice for me. I was going to wear the jeans Mimi had given me, the yellow blouse and my black shoes.

"Why don't you buy something new from Jeans-Jeans?" asked Bea.

"I don't need to."

"You should buy the red T-shirt with Diva written in silver."

I remembered the T-shirt hanging on the rack at Jeans-Jeans. It would be perfect for the show, but the yellow blouse was fine, too.

"It's at least 100,000. That to me is a lot of money."

Bea shrugged.

"On Saturday we're going to Faisal's. I have to make a payment," she said. "I'm sure he'll make you a deal you can't turn down."

Bea had surprised me. Without fail she made a small payment every weekend and chipped away at the cost of the shoes. She paid so regularly that Faisal allowed her to take the shoes home before she had paid it all off. I wondered how she was doing it, as she never seemed to have money. Even though she told us all the gossip of the hospital quarters, she was close-mouthed about her money.

Simon, Osi and Jima practiced hard. I was surprised at how much improvement they made. They were so tight and I was singing better than ever and hitting some high notes I had never thought possible.

"That's it, we're in the groove," Simon said. "We're sounding hot, hot, hot!"

We told all our friends we were playing at the concert. Bea and I practiced some intricate dance movements for "Push It," our funkiest number. It would be good to have my best girlfriend with me on stage.

Saturday came around faster than ever. I had told Christine that I wanted to braid my hair so I left at six-thirty instead of eight in the morning. The birds were in the thick of the morning song. My feet brushed the bushes on the side of the road and came away wet. The day felt new and fresh, full of promises.

I sang as I walked. I could have walked all the way to Kejetia but I took the early tro-tro to make good time. At that time of the morning the roads were free, and we sped off with the tro-tro boy hanging off the back bumper, shouting, "Kejetia! Kejetia!" as if anyone doubted that we were headed for Kejetia.

I had my packet of extensions in my basket and I tried to imagine how I would look with braids dangling to my back. I had put my hair in twists to pull out the tight curls and give me more length. Mary the hair braider had said that it was easier to braid extensions on straightened hair.

I worked my way along narrow alleys and found the hair-braiding center of Kumasi. The stalls were set up to display all kinds of hair in plastic wrap, from synthetic plastic hair to real human hair from Asia. Effie said that in Asia, women grew their hair only to cut it off for money.

Mary's stall was large, and she had several girls working for her. There were women and girls sitting on stools with their hair half done. I should have started out earlier.

"You came," she said when I greeted her. She dragged a stool to the entrance of her stall. "Sit down." She handed me a comb. "Undo your twists." She pointed to one of her apprentices. "Ayele will braid your hair for you."

Ayele pulled the strands apart and began to make small partings in my hair. I gritted my teeth as she parted and pulled, combing through my hair.

In spite of her painful fingertips, Ayele was friendly. She chatted as she worked. I found out she was from Accra. Her hands moved swiftly from the back of my head to the front. She had my neck twisted in some strange way to get to the side of my head without changing her position.

When she was done, she untwisted me. My back was stiff, my neck painful and my hair roots were screaming, but when she showed me a mirror, I felt instantly grateful. I could pass for a Somebody, a daddy's daughter whose father owned a car and whose mother had a maid.

"Now, my dear, go and buy some shadda clothes and you'll look better than the great Jemali."

"Oh, Ayele, this is beautiful," I said. "Thanks."

"Don't! Don't say thank you for hair braiding. It is bad luck! They say we won't find husbands if we accept thanks for doing hair. But we can accept money," she said with a wink.

Even Ayele felt I needed new clothes for my new look. I decided to go to Jeans-Jeans after all.

I squeezed past a row of taxis parked by the roadside and arrived at the shop. I went in and looked around for Faisal, but I couldn't find him. There was the red T-shirt on the wall with DIVA written across it in silver glitter. I looked at it, wondering if I had enough courage to ask to try it on.

Would they let me? I remembered my new look. I beckoned to the attendant.

"Can I try this T-shirt and jeans," I asked as boldly as I could.

"I'll get it off the hook for you." I watched and waited as the T-shirt and its hanger were lowered down on a crook straight into my hands. Next I was given the hip-hugging jeans in size 8.

The changing room was toward the back where Faisal's office was located. I stepped into the narrow cubicle and took off my skirt and blouse. I felt cold. I realized I had never changed in a shop before. I hung my clothes on a nail on the wall. Then I pulled on the T-shirt and pants quickly. The shirt hung just short of my bellybutton in that new style I had seen on TV.

I would have to cross the short corridor to find the full-length mirror on the wall. I wondered why the mirror was so strangely placed. Possibly it was a matter of store security because the office window was directly opposite the mirror.

As I looked in the mirror admiring myself, my eyes met Faisal's through the glass.

"Gloria, my friend, you look different. It took me a while to recognize you," he said.

"I'm just trying this on."

"But now you must have it," he said. "It was absolutely made for you."

His office door was open and he stood against the door frame, arms folded across his chest, the beginnings of a smile tugging at his lips.

"Come, Gloria, let's talk," he said, beckoning me to his office.

I followed him breathlessly. He turned and shut the door. For a moment I panicked. It had to be safe inside a shop.

"Where's your friend?" he asked.

"I came by myself. I went to have my hair done," I said, touching my braids.

"Beautiful," he said.

He reached and touched a braid, too. My belly jumped at his touch. I noticed his eyes for the first time. They were speckled green.

"I like you, Gloria. For you, I'll give half price for everything," he said. "You understand?"

He seemed to be searching my face for some response. Bea was right. Faisal really liked me. He reached for a calculator, made some quick calculations and said, "For trousers and top it's 850,000 but you pay only 400,000 cedis."

"But I don't have that."

"Pay small-small, hmm. Just like your friend Beatrice."

I was perspiring on my forehead and nose, and I felt incredibly hot.

"See, I've written your name. Gloria?"

"Gloria Bampo."

"Address?"

"Block D4, Komfo Anokye Doctors' Flats, Bantama Road."

Someone knocked on the door. It was the shop assistant who had helped me.

"Someone is looking for you, sah," he said to Faisal.

Faisal handed me a bag.

"You can put the clothes in this when you change. Next week come and pay something small," he said. "I wait for you."

There was something about the way he rolled his *r* and the look in his eyes that brought the sweat to my armpits. Then he was gone.

I changed back into my regular clothes and left with my new clothes in the bag.

It was on the way that I realized that he had given me all the clothes even without a down payment.

• ELEVEN •

Christine had just started me on the Level Four series. The letters were smaller, and there were at least ten times more words on a page. I struggled to keep my mind from wandering.

My new clothes were hidden at the bottom of my bag, the one with the broken zipper. I had managed to smuggle them in unnoticed, and the bag was stuffed in the corner of the wardrobe where I hung my clothes.

I got up for the twentieth time to take another peek at the T-shirt and jeans. I was going to wear them next Saturday for the concert. Dark glasses would complete the image. Yes!

I heard the theme song for the Osofo Dadzie show through the open door. "We are going...heaven knows where we are going..."

"Go-go," Sam called. The song was his signal to find me. I loved Osofo Dadzie.

"Glo-glo, are you forgetting Osofo Dadzie?" Christine asked.

"I'm coming, Sistah."

"Reading fever has come over you, eh?" she said as I sat down in front of the TV. Sam got off his mother and climbed on my knee.

"I really want to know English," I said.

We watched the TV and laughed together as Super OD destroyed the English language with mispronunciations and poor grammar. We laughed to burst our sides when Kwadwo Kwakye called his dog Barbara Bush.

"In Europe, with a show like this, they would all be millionaires," said Christine.

"And they can't even speak English right," I said.

"English is important. That group would have traveled the world if they could make people laugh the same way in English. As stupid as it sounds, this language makes all the difference in Ghanaian life — who you'll associate with, which kind of person you're likely to marry, where you can travel, what kind of opportunities your kids will have. It's amazing what reading and writing somebody's language can do for you in this strange world."

How true, I thought. English was the difference between the Somebodies who lived in the suburbs of the cities and the Nobodies of the many villages between Accra and Kumasi.

Christine was not finished yet.

"Take your friend, Bea. If she goes ahead to achieve her dreams as a doctor and you don't study anymore, you'll find yourself calling her Sistah Bea or Auntie Bea."

"Aaah, I'll never call her Sistah Bea," I protested.

"I'm just saying, Glo. I have cousins who are much older than me in my hometown, but when they see me now, they call me Sistah because I'm educated and they are not."

"I'll be Somebody, too," I said.

"Just so you know you have to work at it. It used to be society was divided into royalty and common people, but now the new royalty are the educated."

I thought about that for a while. There had to be other ways than a read-and-write education to find the good life. I could become a talented singing artist like Jemali, or I could become an exceptional dressmaker who sewed only for the rich people of Accra or Kumasi.

Best of all, I could marry someone wealthy.

"Come, let's see your hair," Christine said.

I set Sam on the ground and knelt before Christine. She parted my extensions.

"*Shiee*, how she pulled on your scalp! This is how people lose their hair. You always have to remind the hair braiders to soften their hold, otherwise you'll end up with alopecia and you'll lose your hairline. Does it hurt?"

I nodded.

"Bring the Dax pomade and I'll oil your scalp for you."

I sat at Christine's feet and lay my head on her knee as she began to rub my sore scalp with Dax pomade. Sometimes she stopped as the action on Osofo Dadzie mounted. It was one of those popular TV plays where a poor humble girl becomes rich through meeting a rich man and thereafter becomes incredibly arrogant. Of course we were waiting for the imminent downfall of Baby Nayoka, the star of the show.

"Mamama milk, Go-go milk," Sam pleaded. "Go-go, milk, milk, milk!" he screamed.

"Sam, don't keep shouting at Gloria, otherwise she'll go away," said Christine.

"Sistah, I never want to go back to my home."

I wasn't sure why I said that. Perhaps it was Christine's soft fingertips against my scalp. Perhaps it was the strength of her legs supporting me while my legs supported Sam. Maybe it was the way my world had opened up ever since I had moved to Kumasi.

"I always want to stay here with you," I said.

Christine was quiet. Only her fingers worked against my scalp.

At last she said, "Nothing remains the same forever, Glo."

At the next break in the program, I got up to make Sam's milk. Suddenly I wanted to confide in Christine about the hidden clothes. I returned with Sam's bottle.

"Sistah, I — "

"Glo, next year when Sam goes to preschool I would like you to go back to school to pass your JSS exams."

Me, go back to school? I didn't mind learning to read with Christine, but I didn't want to return to schools and uniforms again.

"Yes, Sistah," I said politely. And the moment for telling about my new clothes passed.

•

Christine left on Thursday instead of Friday. Joe was going to Accra and offered to drive them in his much larger Camry. Because she left on Thursday, I had to miss youth meeting, which meant I had to miss practice.

I didn't worry too much. I felt confident about our performance, but I knew Simon would be unhappy. He was bound to come by later just to get me to sing through the songs. He was so particular.

Christine left the house upside down as she hurried to pack everything she might need in Accra. I'd have to tidy things up and separate the dirty things for washing.

"I have asked Mimi to keep an eye on you for the weekend, Glo, so be good," she said. "She has a bed for you to sleep on. Be as helpful as you can."

"Yes, Sistah." I wasn't afraid to sleep in our apartment by myself, but I guess Christine thought it would be better for me to be supervised.

The car drove off with all my favorite people — Sam, Christine and Dr. Joe, and there was Doyoe in the front seat. Perhaps Doyoe and Joe were solving their problems.

I waved hard and long. I waved until the dust settled on the driveway. Then I returned to our apartment to clean up. I thought I'd tidy the house that night and then go to Mimi's the next morning, as there was so much to do.

I began in Christine's bedroom. I folded her clothes and arranged her shoes on the rack. I shut the drawers and dusted the dresser. Then I took the dirty things and stuffed them in the laundry basket. There would be enough time to wash everything.

I opened her jewelry box and replaced her earrings. And the thought occurred to me that I could use her large earrings and her long heavy chain on stage, as well as her large red bangles. And there was her array of lipsticks and blushes on her make-up tray.

I sat on the stool in front of her vanity and began to apply make-up. First I applied the packed foundation over my face with a piece of foam. I tried to make my eyebrows lush and bold and used the glossiest red lipstick on my lips. I combed my eyelashes through with mascara, making them long and black. I smiled wickedly and made faces at the mirror, trying to look sophisticated, then cute, then coy and sexy. I thought I could pass for twenty or just about, very much like the nurses from the training school who came to the clubhouse with their doctor friends for drinks.

I couldn't wait to show Effie how much her baby sister had grown. She'd be surprised to see my hair in extensions.

When the doorbell rang, I froze.

It couldn't be Christine, I thought. She would have opened the door with her own key. I looked through the window to check anyway. I didn't see Dr. Joe's car. It was probably only Simon coming to make me practice.

When I opened the door it was Bea.

"Gloria, where is Dr. Christine?" she asked, taking in my new look.

"She's gone to Accra. I'm only playing with some make-up."

"Can I try, too?"

I thought for a moment. Christine would not expect me to take Bea to her bedroom. But then she'd never know.

I was feeling silly.

"Come in, young lady. Won't you have a drink?" I put on what I thought was a good British accent.

"Yes, please, lime cordial, please." Then she sat down like a lady and crossed her legs. I served her chemicals, yellow for lime, and it was cold and sweet.

Bea did not drink like a lady. She gulped it all down. Then she let out a large burp.

"Can I powder my nose?" she asked.

"Of course, follow me." I led her to Christine's room and straight to her vanity table. There I dropped my character and said, "*Nsee whee*. Don't mess things up!"

For one hour we tried every look we could imagine, changing eyeshadow colors from red to ice blue and gold. We changed lipstick and applied blush, and Bea styled my braids in different ways. Bea's hair was schoolgirl short, and there wasn't much we could do about that. Christine did not wear wigs and so Bea practiced with head ties and combs.

"Bea, I have something to show you, wait here," I said.

I dashed into my room and reached into the far corner of the wardrobe for my bag. I took off my dress and pulled my Diva T-shirt gently over my head. I pulled the slim-fit jeans over my hips. Then I put on my pumps and rushed back.

"You got it!" Bea exclaimed.

"Christine got it for me," I lied. "I'm wearing it on Saturday."

"Will you let me wear it sometimes?" she asked.

"Okay," I shrugged.

"I want to dress up, too," she said.

"I can't give you Christine's clothes." Make-up was one thing, but I didn't want to open Christine's wardrobe. Bea pouted.

I was wondering what to do when the doorbell rang.

"It must be Simon," I said, running to open the door.

But it was the doctor who had asked my name twice. Dr. Joe's friend.

"Good evening," I stammered.

He stood for a moment staring.

"Good evening," he replied. "I have forgotten your name."

"Gloria."

"Ah, Gloria. Where is your madam?"

"My sister's gone to Accra."

"Do you know where I can find Joe?"

"Dr. Joe has also gone to Accra," I said.

"That explains it. He hasn't answered my calls."

I stood at the door respectfully.

"So you have the whole house then," he said with a smile.

"I'll be staying at Sistah Mimi's," I said carefully.

Then as he turned away, he said, "If you need something, just come to me. I'm in Block E — E6. My name is Kusi, Dr. Kwabena Kusi."

"Thank you," I said.

As soon as I shut the door Bea came from the dining room.

"Was that Dr. Kusi? I hear he's so rich," she said.

"So?"

"What do you mean, *so*? Do you think Dr. Kusi likes you? You're so proud, Gloria."

"I'm not like that, Bea."

"Yes, you are. You think you're so pretty just because Simon and Faisal fuss over you. And just because Christine got you a T-shirt and jeans you think you're something. You can pretend she is your sister, but nobody believes you. You do all the work and she pays you nothing and all you keep saying is she's your sister."

"She is my sister," I shouted. "You're just jealous."

"You're just stupid," she said. "And besides, I saw all those class one books on your bed."

"They are Sam's," I lied.

Bea just laughed. Then she walked out of our apartment and slammed the door.

Tears flooded my eyes.

"I'll never speak to you again," I shouted. But she was already gone.

I changed out of my clothes and washed my face. I tidied Christine's vanity and swept her room. I thought of all Bea's hard words and remembered that I owed Faisal 400,000 cedis that I had no means of paying.

What was I going to do?

The doorbell rang again. It was Simon. Even though I was very unhappy, I sang through every song. I had been looking forward to his visit but now I had no joy.

"What's wrong? You're so quiet," he said. I knew he wanted to stay longer. We'd never had a whole room to ourselves before. But I was not in the mood and I shrugged his arm off my shoulder.

"Bea and I have quarreled, so she won't be dancing with me," I said. "I don't want her in the group."

• TWELVE •

I woke up nervous. I put it down to the quarrel with Bea but I knew it was also the show.

What if I forgot the words or sang off tune or missed my cues? What if I let our band down? I wished Bea was going to be with me after all, just as we had practiced.

I went downstairs to Mimi's apartment in the morning and we had breakfast together. She fried eggs and afterward I helped her tidy her house. Then I went back to our apartment to get ready for the afternoon.

By one o'clock I was all dressed up. I wanted blue eyeshadow for my eyes, but I couldn't find Christine's so I settled on green. Bea and I had planned to meet the guys at two at the cultural center, but I left by myself, carrying uneasiness in my belly like a hundred worms. The show would start at four.

I stepped into the bushes to make room for the car behind me, but instead of passing, it slowed to a stop, its engine purring like a cat.

It was a red Passat. The front passenger window went down as if by magic.

I looked through it. It was Dr. Kusi.

"Where are you going?" he asked. "I'll give you a ride. Hop in."

It was good to get a ride in an air-conditioned car at two o'clock when the sun was at its worst. I told him I was singing with my band at the Anansekrom at the cultural center.

"Wow, then I'm coming to watch."

I wondered if he meant it. Neither Mimi nor Julie was coming as they were both on duty.

"It starts at four," I said as we whizzed through town. He stopped at the gates of the cultural center and let me out.

"You're looking good," he said. "So beautiful."

"Thanks."

"See you then."

Outside a crowd was building up quickly. It was a sweltering hot day and even the flies were slow and fatigued. Thankfully I found Osi and Jima right away. Then Simon came through the gates and led us in to the back of the stage where all the performers were gathering. The F Block guys were all dressed in black T-shirts and jeans.

"You're looking handsome," I said. There were high fives all around.

"*Wo ye blade,*" Jima said.

"Yes, you're sharp," said Osi. And Simon gave me a hug.

We waited our turn at the sound check while the other bands tried the microphones and the stage. Meanwhile, the crowd assembled on the grass. It was rowdy at the gates as ticket holders struggled through the dense crowd of people wanting tickets. I wondered if Dr. Kusi had made it.

By the time the show started it was about five-thirty. Our MC was Wonder Mike, the popular radio DJ with the put-on American accent, with slurred r's and a nasal twang. The crowd was going crazy. Then the bands began to play.

Suddenly we were mounting the steps to the stage. Simon was strapping on his guitar, Osi was fingering his piano keys, and I found the microphone and worked it off the stand. And there was Bea suddenly, in blue jeans and a red Diva shirt just like mine.

"Sorry about yesterday, Glo," she said. "I don't want to let the band down."

Then I heard Simon's voice on the microphone.

"Hello Kumasi, hello Anansekrom, this is F Block of Bantama Kumasi with our first song, 'Push It.' One, two, three, four." And we charged into the first song with everything we had. Bea and I performed a flawless choreography between verses of rap carried by Simon and me. The crowd joined in the chorus with shouts of "Push it hard, push it right, push at it with all your might."

The rest of our show passed like a blur. I didn't want to stop.

This was it! Show biz! I wished Effie could have seen me. Afterward we hugged each other. It felt like we would never let each other go.

•

Christine returned with Sam Wednesday afternoon on the bus. I thought they were coming back with Dr. Joe, but Dr. Joe was on leave for a whole month and had left Accra for London, England. He hadn't even told me that he wasn't going to be back for four whole weeks.

Christine was tired. She didn't talk much even when Julie and Mimi came over for her news. I had fresh squeezed orange juice chilling in the fridge and served it up in tall slim glasses.

"Have you heard? Glo is our local star. I hear she was wild at the Anansekrom. Kwabena Kusi saw her. He says it was *kra be whe*," said Mimi.

"Does KK still go to these teen things?" asked Julie.

They laughed, but Christine only managed a ghost of a smile. Her friends caught on that she wasn't feeling sociable and left soon after.

Christine's phone rang.

I guessed it was JB.

"Sam, time to bath," I said. I picked him up and held him against my hip. "You're getting heavy."

"Heavy, heavy," he chanted.

I opened the door to the bathroom. Christine's voice sounded as though she was having an argument.

"I don't mind coming for a holiday but I won't be staying. We agreed on one year and I did two. Now it's time for you to come home."

I shut the door quietly. Sam pointed to his yellow plastic ducks and said, "Ducky-ducky."

"I missed you, Sam," I said. "Kiss-kiss?"

He hugged me with his wet arms and kissed me on the cheek. He had missed his Go-go.

I waited for Christine to give me news from Accra, but she didn't want to chat. She said she didn't want a meal so I made sandwiches and tea for supper. Soon after, she took Sam with her to the bedroom. Sometimes she lay by him until he had fallen asleep. Then she would return to the living room to finish some reading or watch TV.

I waited, but Christine did not come back and when I checked on her, she was fast asleep, still dressed for the day. I'd wanted to tell her about our concert but she'd seemed so preoccupied. I also wanted to hear about my family.

Christine was gone all the next morning. She dashed home briefly just to check on Sam and then she returned to work. Her team was on duty and she was responsible for the polyclinic. Only one doctor managed all the walk-ins and all the wound suturing. Usually she had this arrangement with Joe where she went to assist him on his duty days and he assisted her when it was her duty day. But Joe was gone and Christine had to do it on her own.

Sam and I got ready for a walk. Sam wanted to wear a new T-shirt they had brought from Accra.

"Where did you get this?" I asked.

"Dadada."

"Fine shirt, Sam. So handsome," I said.

"So handsome," he replied gleefully.

I dressed him up in the orange Donald Duck shirt and khaki shorts they had brought from Accra. He also had a brand new pair of sneakers. Then I dressed up, too, simply in a skirt and blouse and my favorite shoes that I wore to church. We walked hand in hand along the driveway to the clubhouse.

It was four in the afternoon and there were not many people there yet. I ordered Fanta at the bar. Then we went to sit outside beneath the umbrellas. I had Sam's no-spill beaker, and we shared the bottle between us.

Two women were playing tennis. The women who usually came to the clubhouse were young and dressed to kill, not to sweat. All they did was talk and laugh between sips of ice-cold drinks, groundnuts and kebabs. Watching them closely, I had learned to sip my drink slowly, too.

The doctors were arriving for the afternoon's tennis with their young ladies in their high-heeled sandals and colorful tops and skirts. The two women on the court were playing hard. They were dressed in white shirts, white miniskirts, white socks and white sneakers. They looked middle-aged but they seemed fit. One of the women was fair colored, the kind people called half-caste, with silky curly hair. The other one was fully African.

I didn't know African women played tennis.

I heard one of the men shout a greeting to the curly-haired woman.

"Mrs. Kotoh, how is the good doctor?"

"He's fine," she shouted back. "He's on duty today."

Mrs. Kotoh? I stared at her. It had to be Bea's stepmother.

She was such a pretty woman. I remembered Bea had said she was German. She should have said half German.

"Gloria."

The soft voice belonged to Dr. Kusi.

"I saw your show at Anansekrom. You were fabulous," he said.

I smiled. Sam was trying hard to get off my lap. I bounced him up and down to amuse him. It wouldn't do to have him running on the court.

"You did so well, I got you a gift. Come by sometime and get it."

"Thanks," I said.

"Here, have this. Buy Sam a drink." Just for one drink at 1,000 cedis, he had placed 20,000 cedis on our table.

"Keep the change," he said.

I picked up the money before the wind could blow it away. I remembered Faisal's clothes and the money I owed.

"Thank you very much," I said.

"Any time," he replied. Then he joined his friends.

At Dr. Kusi's table all the men wore white shirts and shorts, and they all carried white towels around their necks. They looked like they had every intention of playing hectic tennis, even though their tables were crowded with beer.

"Drink, drink," shouted Sam.

"It's enough," I said to Sam. "You'll have a tummy ache." But Sam only shouted louder.

"Go-go, Sprite! Sprite!" he demanded.

"Don't be wicked. Get him a drink," said Dr. Kusi

loudly from among his friends. I laughed along with them.

"Wiki-wicki Go-go," said Sam.

"See what you've done," I said.

We were all laughing when the women finished their game and returned to their table. I stood Sam up and took his hand. It was time to leave.

"Nice baby," said one of the women tennis players.

"His name is Sam."

"Whose baby is it?" asked Mrs. Kotoh.

"Dr. Christine Ossei."

She poked Sam's cheek and tried to make him laugh.

"Sam, say bye," I said politely.

"Bye," said Sam waving at them. Ever since Sam had discovered the wave, he was so happy to use it for everyone. He waved until they were out of our sight.

Out on the path I saw Bea on her way into town. Our eyes locked for a moment. I noticed she had blue eyeshadow around her eyes. She was wearing a belt we had seen in Faisal's shop and a really nice dress. Even her hair seemed a little bushier.

I was going to say hello but she turned away. Had she made peace with me only because she'd wanted to sing with F Block?

My fingers curled around the 20,000 cedi bill that Dr. Kusi had given me. I hoped this was the beginning of exceeding good luck.

• THIRTEEN •

September brought in the rain. In Kumasi the downpours were heavy, drenching those victims caught outside within mere seconds of an inciting thunderclap. Umbrellas were useless, so when the rain came down, people found shelter and stayed put until the storm was over.

It was also the start of the school year and so my friends came around less. As for Bea, she no longer visited, and it seemed as if that single quarrel had wrecked our friendship permanently.

Christine brought me a pink blouse from Accra. She also brought me greetings from Auntie Ruby, Effie, Daa and Maa.

"Ah, Glo, I forgot to give you your parcel from home and it's been a whole week," she said as she ate the last morsel of her fried yam before going to work in the afternoon. She went back to her bedroom and brought me a bulky brown envelope. My father's name, Mr. J.A.K. Bampo, had been crossed out and replaced with GLORIA in red ink.

Daa had sent me a Gideon's pocket New Testament

with instructions through Christine that I read it every day. Effie's letter was in a beautiful pink floral envelope.

"Aren't you going to open it?" Christine asked as I turned the letter around in my hand.

"I will."

"I can help you," said Christine.

"I'll read it," I insisted.

The night before, I had tried to read Effie's first letter. Although I could read some words, I had not understood her note. I had made a new goal. I was going to wait until I could read at Level Ten. Then I'd open the other letters, read them and reply to them all by myself. One day I would write a perfect letter to my friends who had gone on to senior secondary school. The thought pleased me.

There was a bit of trouble between Christine and JB. That was why she had hardly spoken about her trip to Accra. Christine no longer seemed excited when he called. Her voice was tense, her sentences clipped. I thought of Dr. Joe and Doyoe, and I was very worried for Christine and JB.

One Saturday I went to the market to buy foodstuffs. I found Ayele the hair braider at the entrance.

I left my basket with her and rushed off to Faisal's, my heart beating rapidly, my sandals flopping at my heels. I no longer wore slippers to the market. Sandals looked a whole lot better and I never carried my basket on my head anymore.

Faisal was in the shop talking to some clients. He was looking fine in dark brown trousers and an immaculate white T-shirt and shiny black leather shoes. There was a gold chain around his neck.

"Come, Gloria," he said when he saw me. And I followed him to his office in the back.

"I have some money," I said, opening my purse to take out the 20,000 that Dr. Kusi had given me. I reached across the table with the money. Faisal took the money and my hand.

"Thank you," he said.

My hand was still in his. He slid his other hand up my arm and I remembered the man who had grabbed my hand when I was selling oranges, but I wasn't afraid.

Faisal's face was gentle.

"You wore the clothes, yes?" he asked.

I nodded.

"You didn't come to show me," he chided. He looked at me thoughtfully and a smile turned up the corners of his lips. "You have a boyfriend?"

I hesitated. Simon was like my boyfriend, but it was hard to say it.

At last he let me go. He opened his ledger and made an entry. Then he handed me a receipt for 20,000 cedis.

"Maybe, sometime, I come to find you," he said.

I laughed. Then I remembered he had my address.

"You know the Lebanon Club?"

I shook my head. I didn't know Kumasi well at all, but Bea would know for sure.

"It's close to the hospital," he said. "Friday afternoons we play basketball. Maybe you like to watch?"

"I don't know," I said.

"You like music, kebabs and drinks?"

I nodded.

"Friday, hmm? Come and watch me play." Faisal laughed, showing white gleaming teeth. "I give you something." He pulled a drawer open and gave me a silver frosted belt with a large sequined buckle. He also gave me a small plastic bag to carry it in.

"Thank you very much," I said. "I have to go now."

"Don't forget, Friday at five-thirty." Then he blew me a kiss, just like in the films.

I hurried back to Ayele for my basket. On a whim I decided to buy a whole lot of cassava and large apantu plantains to make fufu.

We never made fufu at the apartment. Christine didn't even have a mortar and pestle. But downstairs, Dr. Owusu's wife made fufu every day.

It wasn't that Christine didn't like fufu, but whenever they wished for it, Dr. Joe would take her to the Scoreboard chop-bar, where the fufu was declared to be the best. Sometimes she bought fufu at the nearby Ghana-Guinea-Mali restaurant.

The craving for fufu and groundnut soup was sudden and strong, so I rearranged my list and bought everything I needed. I followed my nose to where the mudfish was arranged on wooden trays, blackened with smoke. I bought tolo-beef steeped in salt and four cups of groundnut paste, which the lady wrapped in leaves. I filled my basket until I could barely lift it, but I managed to drag it off to the taxi rank. This time, without Bea, the taxi driver drove me all the way to D Block.

Christine said there was a rule at the doctors' flats that we couldn't pound fufu on the higher floors, so I went down to the ground floor and asked Mrs. Owusu if I could pound fufu on their back porch with her mortar and pestle.

Everyone passing by saw me on my kitchen stool pounding fufu. Just a half hour into the process, I had said yes to several people who asked for a taste of the food when it was done. Mostly this meant nothing except friendly conversation. After all, I didn't cook for myself. I cooked for Christine. I had suggested to Christine that we invite her friends Julie and Mimi to dinner.

Bea passed by dressed up as if she had a party to attend. She was with a group, some of whom I recognized from the complex. I wondered if Bea still had it in mind to become a doctor. Certainly she was gallivanting more than ever.

On an impulse I shouted her name. She turned and waved.

"I'll be back," she said. She sounded friendly.

"I'll be waiting for you," I said. I resumed pounding with even more vigor.

The fufu became softer under my pounding as people passed to and fro. Then I saw Dr. Kusi walking up the path on his way to the carport.

"Gloria, I didn't know you were strong enough to pound fufu with one hand and turn it with the other."

"I'm strong," I said, laughing.

"I want to taste your food," he said.

"I'll save you some," I promised. "I owe you thanks."

"No problem there."

"Everybody's talking about your car."

"Do you like it?"

"Yes. It's very nice. It makes the road as smooth as water."

"I'll take you and Sam for a long ride soon."

"Okay," I said.

"I'll be waiting for the fufu." And as he strode off he added, "I mean it."

At last the fufu was ready and I arranged the balls in a large serving dish. The soup was simmering on the stove and the aroma wafted to meet me as I climbed the stairs. Julie and Mimi were chatting upstairs in the living room with Christine, and Sam was riding his car around the apartment.

"Glo, we aren't even going to take a drink before we've eaten," said Julie.

"I'm hugging my belly until you've fed us," said Mimi.

"If I know Glo well, she's invited the whole compound," said Julie. "It's in our interest to begin eating right away."

I laughed and dished the food out into bowls, making sure to save some for Dr. Kusi. I announced that Sam was going to eat fufu for the first time in his life. His soup stood apart in a little saucepan. I had added mashed carrots and no pepper at all. I had also boiled a whole egg for him.

They trooped off to wash their hands in the kitchen sink. Fufu was meant to be eaten only one way, fingers pinching off bits of soft mash, dipped into bowls of soup and allowed to slip gently down waiting throats.

We all sat down to eat. Christine said a prayer and dished out the soup. Everyone dug in. Sam was so funny with his face all scrunched up. He didn't like the fufu but he liked the groundnut soup. So Christine mixed in Farex baby rice flakes and made a thick paste for him.

We ate without speaking much except for the grunts of appreciation.

"What would we do without you, Glo?" Julie said at least three times.

"Don't swell her head with your praises," said Christine.

The phone rang. Christine used her good hand to answer it. It was JB. They spoke for a short while.

"I'll call you later," said Christine. "I have guests and we're eating Gloria's fufu."

She laughed at something JB said. "Later. Bye."

She was chewing the last of the meat off the bones. The bones were soft and full of flavor, and I had already chewed mine to bits, sucking up all the marrow.

"JB's jealous of our fufu," she said.

"How's he doing?" Julie asked.

"He's okay. He wants to work in the UK for a few more years, and he wants me to move back with Sam. We've had so many arguments lately. I almost want to tell him to stay there if he wants to," said Christine. "In the beginning, we agreed on my spending one year there. I ended up spending two."

"But, Christine, you wouldn't just sit home next time. You could specialize in pediatrics," said Julie.

"I didn't like England. I'd much rather stay here. We shouldn't have married if he was going to turn everything around on me," said Christine.

I fed Sam all his food and he cleaned out his plate. I was as quiet as a ghost.

"Good boy," I whispered when he was done.

Christine turned to me and said, "Glo, please clear the plates."

I could tell she had forgotten about me as she spoke with her friends. She probably wished I hadn't heard what she'd said. Who wouldn't want to go and live in Europe? I had heard the shops were full to overflowing and everybody owned a car, a Walkman and good clothes. I was quite sure that in the end Christine would agree to go. After all, wives were supposed to obey their husbands.

Suddenly it occurred to me that if they left for England, she might take me to look after Sam. *Shiee!* That would be amazing. I would pray hard for that to happen.

I washed the plates and set them on the draining board. I looked at the remaining fufu in the bowls I had set aside. I decided to take Dr. Kusi his portion as I had promised.

I heated up the soup quickly and dished a few ladles into an enamel bowl with a fitted plastic lid. I covered the fufu with a good selection of beef, smoked mudfish and dried herring. Then I placed the bowl in a nice round basket and covered it with a tea cloth.

Christine and her friends were still talking. I dashed out quickly. I would only be a couple of minutes. Block E was just around the corner.

Dr. Kusi opened the door of his apartment. Music was playing loudly from his entertainment center displaying a large TV and a stacked sound system. I saw that he had been studying at his dining-room table, because the books were open and a reading lamp had been switched on. Otherwise the room was quite dark.

"Gloria, come in, come in," he said pleasantly.

He was wearing khaki shorts and a singlet. I saw the tight hairs on his chest and strong shoulders. He wasn't as built up as Dr. Joe, but he looked strong.

"I brought you some fufu and soup and I have to go right away."

"You're always in a hurry, but at least you came today. I'll tell you tomorrow how much I like your handwriting."

I knew he was talking about my cooking. His voice was so soft.

"Bye," I said, and I ran down the stairs and all the way home. I was back in our kitchen again when I remembered I had left the basket and tea cloth.

The women were still talking and no one had missed me. The TV was on and a cartoon was playing for Sam. I went to my bedroom and took out Book 4C. I began to practise my reading.

If we were going to England I would have to know English well. In England I might even be happy to return to school. I could become a nurse or a designer or a singer. Maybe I could even become a doctor.

Anything was possible.

• FOURTEEN •

Christine always drank tea before she left for work in the morning. I knew exactly how she liked it — strong, thick with Ideal milk and two cubes of sugar. If she had time, I made her chi-bom, omelet with fried tomatoes and peppers. Most mornings she had to leave by 7:45 to get to the wards by eight. On Wednesdays, when she had rounds and mortality meetings, she left by 7:15.

But this Wednesday morning her meetings went better than she had expected, and she returned in a good mood. She even baked a cake. Baking was something I knew nothing about, so I watched everything that Christine did, from creaming the margarine and sugar to breaking in eggs and folding in the flour. Afterward I ate the remains of the mixture in the bowl. It was almost as good as the cake itself.

On Thursday morning Christine said to me that Sam had been invited to play with Mrs. Owusu's daughter. Elizabeth Owusu was five years old and completely in love with Sam, always wanting to hold him in a tight hug. I knew that Sam would spend the entire morning running away from her.

Christine left while Sam was still asleep, and I prayed. I prayed that Christine would agree to go to England and take me along. Then I prayed for Effie, Maa and Daa. But I didn't read my new Bible.

I washed Sam's diapers while he slept. I was hanging them on the line on our balcony to dry when I heard a hiss from the carport.

It was Dr. Kusi. He waved.

"Gloria, I will be back at noon. Come and see me."

How perfect. I would be able to collect the basket and cloth before Christine came back at two.

Mrs. Owusu gave us Piccadilly biscuits. She gave Sam Golden Tree chocolates and filled their cups with chemicals. It was like a birthday party. I was worried that he was having too many sweets, but he was happy, so I let him play with Elizabeth and eat all the things that Christine called junk.

At twelve o'clock, I told her I had some chores to do.

"I'll watch Sam," she said. "I'm making jolof and I'll feed him, too. Go and do your chores."

Dr. Kusi had said noon, and there was his red car in his regular parking spot.

I walked over to E Block, climbed to the third floor and knocked on his door.

He opened it. His curtains were drawn and the room was dark. The music that came from his speakers was slow. Dr. Kusi was dressed for work in a white shirt and tie. He looked quite handsome, and I'd never thought of him as handsome.

"Gloria, come in," he said. "Your food was so good. I took it into my dreams and feasted all night."

"Thank you," I said.

"I kept your basket for you," he said, pointing to the basket on his dining table.

"Thank you."

"Sit down," he said. "Do you ever watch movies? I have some great movies."

Dr. Kusi's television was large, and the picture extremely good. He searched through his videos and found one. He turned off his music and started the video.

"Sit there," he said, pointing to the couch. "That's the best spot for viewing."

I sat down as if on a nest full of eggs, and the movie began. Dr. Kusi brought me a glass of Sprite and placed it on the coffee table by my side.

"I can only stay for an hour," I said. I sat alone watching. I supposed Dr. Kusi was doing some work in his bedroom. Christine also kept a desk in her room for her work.

I sipped my drink and got caught up in the action. How did he know that I liked Indian movies? I had never seen this one before. It was called *Yaadon Ki Baaraat*, and the actors were beautiful in flowing shiny silks in bold reds and greens, beautifully embroidered with golden thread. Indian movie stars were the most beautiful, and their make-up was gorgeous.

At some time during the movie, Dr. Kusi returned and sat by me. I felt his thigh against mine. He put an arm around me, and his voice when he spoke my name was velvet.

I trembled. I smelled his perfume and a whiff of alcohol.

The next thing I knew, his lips were on my ear. Then he found my lips and kissed me. I sat as still as a rock. His hands felt my breasts.

"I love you, Gloria," he said as he kissed me lightly over my face, my cheeks and my forehead. He kissed my lips, pushing his tongue into my mouth.

The movie ended and the room filled with silence. He withdrew, his large eyes fixed intently on me.

"There's something about you, Gloria. You're young but there's something special about you."

His words felt good. He returned to kissing and caressing me, and his hands were soft. His breath on my face tickled, and I began to kiss him back.

"Thank you for the food," he said a little while later. "If you were a little older, I'd marry you. But now I'll have to wait for you. Can you wait for me?" His voice was softer than ever. "Will you wait for me, my love?"

His words overwhelmed me. I sat drinking them in, falling in love with him as I sat on the gray couch in flat E6. It was like a dream. He caressed my face and his finger lingered over my lips.

"Wait, little wife," he said.

He kissed me again lightly on the lips.

"There is a gift for you in the basket," he said. "Don't tell anyone about it."

"Thank you," I said in a whisper.

He smiled. "It's because I love you. I have felt something special for you ever since I saw you at the clubhouse that day."

I don't know how I got back to D4. My legs were wobbly and my belly felt hollow. I wondered if this was the sin Daa called licentiousness.

Back at home, I found a thick wad of notes under the folded tray cloth in my basket. I sat on the bed and counted the money.

It was 350,000 cedis. I had never had so much money in my life.

I found my bag with the broken zipper and stuffed the money deep in the bag. On Saturday I would pay Faisal and owe only 30,000 cedis.

I replaced the red Diva T-shirt and blue jeans in the bag, covering the money. Then I stuffed in my old clothes, my letters and my books.

It occurred to me that I needed to buy a good bag with a lock, because now I had secrets to keep.

•

On Friday afternoon, Bea came to my house after school. It was the first time we had visited in weeks. We sat uncomfortably for a few minutes. I wanted to tell her about Dr. Kusi but I held back. Dr. Kusi had sparked the strange quarrel between Bea and me.

"Gloria, I wanted to invite you to my confirmation party two weeks Saturday," she said.

"Where?"

"At the clubhouse," she replied. "Two o'clock."

"Bea, you were so nasty the other day. You never even apologized. Then you just ignored me for weeks. I thought we were friends."

"I said hello to you the other day."

"But you never said sorry."

"I did say sorry at Anansekrom, but if that wasn't enough, then *sorry*," she said at last.

I wanted to ask her why she had been so nasty but I thought better of it. Saying sorry was hard enough for Bea.

"I'm glad we're friends again," I said.

"Me, too," she replied, and she raised her right hand up for a high five. It was nice to slap hands.

On Saturday I paid Faisal, and he handed me another receipt and a gift. This time it was a small handbag. Again he invited me to his club to watch basketball. I said that I was usually busy on Fridays.

"I'll wait for you, my friend," he said, patting my cheek. And the smile never left his face.

•

September meant that Simon had begun SSS3, his final and most important year in secondary school. The senior exams were difficult, and if Simon wanted to study engineering at the university, he'd have to work very hard to pass his exams well. F Block had not met since the show at Anansekrom. Add on the disruptions due to the rain, and we hadn't met for weeks.

Ever since Dr. Kusi had kissed me, I wasn't sure what to do about Simon. I liked him a lot, but Dr. Kusi made me feel different. Just thinking about him made me feel hollow in my belly.

Christine was still having arguments with JB. I prayed that they would be happy again. I prayed that I would learn to read quickly. I also prayed blessings for my family in Accra.

Thursday came around. We needed to wake up our band if it was going to live.

I dressed up and kissed Sam goodbye. I stopped by Bea's house but no one was in so I walked up the driveway and was nearly at the main road when I heard the familiar purr of a car behind me.

My heart skipped as the red Passat stopped beside me and the dark-toned window went down smoothly into the door.

"Little wife," said Dr. Kusi.

I wasn't sure how to answer so I laughed.

"Sit down," he said. "I'll drive you."

So I got into the car and shut the door gently. It was such a beautiful car. The seats were made of black leather, soft and deep. The dashboard was jet black with red and green lights blinking. Lionel Richie's "Stuck on You" played softly as the air-conditioning bathed us in cool air. I lay back against the headrest, glad that the windows were darkened.

"Where are you going?" he said.

"To youth meeting at the Redeemer Baptist Church."
Dr. Kusi drove fast.

"When does the meeting start?" he asked.

"At six o'clock."

"When does it end?"

"Eight o'clock. Sometimes I go earlier when we have
band practice."

"There's enough time to show you something interesting."

The car rode smoothly along the road from Bantama
to Asafo, and we gained speed as our single lane road
gave way to a dual-carriage highway.

"On the right is the university," he said. "Next time I'll
bring you here to show you around. That's where most of
the doctors at the complex studied."

He fiddled with some knobs on the console, and
Lionel Richie gave way to Daddy Lumba, who sang of
betrayed love.

"I love Daddy Lumba," I said. I sang along, and Dr.
Kusi's voice joined mine for the chorus.

"Lovely voice," he said.

"Thank you."

"What did you buy for yourself?" he asked when the
song ended.

"I got a T-shirt and jeans."

"You look good in jeans," he said. "I like those ones
you wore for the Anansekrom show."

"Did you really watch?"

"Sure. Your band was the best."

"We haven't practiced for a while, but we will have to work hard if we want to be professional. Then we will record our own CD," I said.

"You'll need some sponsorship, hmm?"

"That's what Simon says."

"I'll see what can be done about that."

Wait until I tell Simon, I thought. Then it occurred to me that Simon might not be that excited after all. Simon liked me.

"Those jeans you bought, you should wear for me sometime," he said.

I nodded. I didn't tell him he'd already seen them.

"Like I said before, if you need anything at all, just ask."

"Thank you," I said. I wasn't used to asking. I had only ever taken what I was given.

We drove out of town and the music played, soft and gentle. We drove past some villages and kept going.

"Where are we going?" I asked. It seemed as though we were traveling to Accra.

"Right here."

He turned into a dusty driveway. For a moment I thought we were headed into the forest. I remembered the stories I had grown up with about handsome men turning into snakes in the forest and eating up foolish young women who thought they were in love.

But we didn't enter the forest. What stood before us was a beautiful building.

"It's a new hotel. I wanted to buy you a meal and spend some time with you." He stopped the car. "Do you believe me when I say I love you?"

I nodded.

"Do you love me?"

I nodded.

"Say it," he demanded.

"I love you," I said. I was completely overwhelmed by all the emotion between us.

We drew closer. I felt drawn to his eyes and I couldn't look away.

"Say my name," he said.

"Dr. Kusi."

"No. Call me Kwabena."

"Kwabena," I whispered.

"Say, Kwabena, I love you."

"Kwabena, I love you."

Tears filled my eyes and my voice broke for no reason at all. He engulfed me within his arms. He kissed me for an eternity.

"This love between you and me is like magic. It's made in heaven, but if you tell anyone before it is time, it will break and disappear." His voice was so solemn, so serious. It seemed as though he might cry from the fear of our love disappearing into thin air. "I give you my heart, Gloria. Keep it well. I give you my confidence. Keep it well." He took my hand and placed it on his chest, where his heart was beating furiously. "See what you do to me?"

I nodded, overwhelmed.

We ate Chinese fried rice and spring rolls. He drank wine but I drank Sprite as usual.

Then he took me to a room. The bed was perfectly made with clean white sheets.

"Come," he said, lying down.

I went and sat on the edge of the bed, but he drew me down beside him.

I closed my eyes. Then I remembered the man in Accra who had grasped my wrist in his hand. How fast I had run then. But now I felt cornered by Kwabena Kusi's gentle words.

His hands were stroking me. Then suddenly I felt his weight on me.

Too late, I thought, feeling very small.

"I love you," he whispered hard into my ear.

Perhaps he really loved me. It was all I could hope for. I clenched my teeth and stilled the fear rising in me.

•

"See, I wore a condom," he said afterward. "I won't get you pregnant. I won't get you into trouble. Trust me, hmm."

I looked at the funny-shaped plastic thing. It was not appealing. I wondered at what I had done. I tried not to think of Daa as I pulled my dress down.

"I look forward to when we can do this freely. I look forward to our babies one day. I look forward to a home with you." His voice was so tender, I wanted to cry. I hoped God would understand. One day I would become Mrs. Kusi and this would be made right.

Dear God, help me, I prayed silently.

We drove back in silence while Lionel Richie played. From time to time, Kwabena Kusi would reach for my hand and hold it. Then he would let it slip gently.

He dropped me outside the church at seven o'clock. When I went inside, I felt sin on my back like a dirty shirt.

• FIFTEEN •

Dr. Joe was gone for a month. When he returned, he brought me a white dress with blue roses, and I loved it. But he was different. Quieter. He no longer laughed from his belly, nor did his smile reach his eyes. Christine said that Joe and Doyoe had broken up for good because Agnes's family had pressured Joe into an engagement. Agnes was the other girl, the one we had met at the club-house.

"You should see how she wears her belly proudly, like an ornament," said Mimi.

"What do you expect when a guy walks around with his macho on his chest?" said Julie. "Don't blame the girl. They deserve each other."

Dr. Julie had no pity, I thought. I was broken-hearted for Doyoe.

Julie was unlike any of the other women doctors. It wasn't just her short hair. She also did not follow Kumasi fashion trends and she didn't go to church. Julie had her own thoughts about everything.

The Saturday came for Agnes and Joe's engagement,

and our compound was buzzing with activity. All the doctors were traveling to Agnes's town to present the marriage drinks. All the trainee nurses were going as well. Dr. Joe's colleagues carried crates of minerals and beer over from the apartments to the waiting cars. Christine said Kwabena Kusi was going to be the spokesman for Joe.

I wanted to go, too. I had never been to an engagement. But mainly I wanted to see Kwabena Kusi perform as okyeame for the occasion.

Christine wanted me to stay home with Sam.

"Let her come," said Julie. "Then she can dream about her own marriage one day." Julie had the funniest ways of saying things.

"Don't put thoughts into her head. Marriage is a long way off," said Christine.

"In the village some people are married at her age."

"This is the city," said Christine. "Here she is still a child."

"Is she?" said Julie.

I watched the doctors pack themselves and their girlfriends into their cars. Christine was driving her Corolla and every seat was taken. Kwabena Kusi packed his car full of his colleagues. His car was easily the best — brand new and shiny. A woman I had never seen before took the front seat where I had twice sat. She was light skinned with silky curly hair. She reminded me of Mrs. Kotoh at the tennis court. I watched quietly.

Kwabena Kusi looked up, saw me on the balcony and waved. I smiled and waved back.

The woman with the curly hair said something to him. She was probably asking who I was. He said something back. The car doors slammed shut.

I'd let others take my seat until I was old enough. I would never break the magic of our love by speaking too soon. I only wished I could tell Effie everything. She would understand.

With most of the doctors gone the complex was quiet. My scalp itched. My extensions were old and messy. I spent the afternoon taking them off while Sam slept. I washed my hair with Christine's shampoo. I was careful not to pour a whole lot. She didn't mind when I used her things but I was careful not to misuse her generosity.

I was stunned at the new length of my hair. One day I would straighten my hair with Ultra Sheen crème relaxer and style it any way I wanted. But not yet — not until I was earning money or married.

I dried my hair and twisted my locks into three-twisted braids. Christine always used her extensions just once and threw them away, but I had taken mine out carefully and washed them. Perhaps next Saturday Ayele would be free to put in new extensions.

Sam woke up. I fed him mash yam and palm nut stew. He stained his shirt with palm oil, so I soaked the shirt in Omo detergent and water. Bea came by wondering what we could do. I had no ideas and I didn't want to go to the clubhouse.

"There's no one there anyway," Bea said. "It's so dead."

I put on a video for Sam and warmed some milk for him. We spent an hour looking through Christine's photo albums. In England, even the buses were two stories high.

"Christine says in England, it can get as cold as our freezer," I said. I opened the freezer and put my hand in there for a few minutes just to feel the winter she talked about. Bea scraped some ice off the sides of the freezer and licked it.

"I want to go to America some day," she said.

"Christine may be going to England soon," I said.

"Will she take you?"

"I hope so."

"You have all the luck."

I didn't tell Bea that Christine did not want to go. "I'm hoping JB agrees to come home soon," she had said. "Europe is not the heaven some make it out to be. It's cold and unfriendly, particularly to Africans. They look down on our skin color and are sometimes very mean toward us."

I didn't believe her. Everybody wanted to go abroad. The people who traveled to Europe came back with good things like clothes, cars and money. In our church back home the monthly all-night meetings were filled with powerful prayers for visas and tickets and scholarships, all for traveling abroad to Europe and America. We hoped our turn would come one day for God's prosperous blessings.

"Do you want me to braid your hair?" Bea asked.

"Can you do Rasta?"

"Yes. Do you have hair extensions? I'll do it for you for free."

"Thanks," I said. I sat on the kitchen stool while Bea braided my hair. It took three hours in all but it was a good job.

When I next saw Bea, it was Monday afternoon. She had on gold eyeshadow, even though she was in her school uniform. Bea told me that her party had been postponed to the end of term in December. She said she had her dress already. She had bought it from another boutique with better things than Jeans-Jeans.

•

JB was coming to visit for two weeks. I was so excited. Every day I talked to Sam about his dad. Every day we walked around the living room. I pointed at the pictures of JB and we sang songs to him.

In the evenings, I read. Christine taught me more about reading and words when she wasn't busy. Sometimes we worked on grammar — past tense, present tense and future tense. I was reading at Level Eight. I was writing good sentences, too. I confided in Christine that my goal was to read the Level Ten book before November ended.

"Then I'll write my sister Effie a letter," I said.

"Go for it, Glo. I'm sure you could write your JSS exams again next year. I don't see why not."

I didn't want to do JSS exams again. I dreamed of visiting England with Christine and Sam, and then marrying Dr. Kusi after I returned.

"Sistah, if you go to London will you take me?" I asked.

"Oh, Glo, if only you knew. It would be so much better if we built up our nation and stayed in it. It would be for our own good."

•

Most Thursdays before youth meeting, Kwabena Kusi picked me up at the roadside and we went away to the hotel in the woods where we made love.

One day, Kwabena asked me how old I was.

"Sixteen and a half."

"We'll wait two years, Gloria. Then you'll be old enough to marry," he said. "It's so hard to wait. I love you so."

I didn't ask him how old he was but I guessed he was between twenty-six and twenty-eight years old. It was hard for me to wait, too. I loved him and I dreamed about him all day. Sometimes I whispered his name to myself. He always filled my purse with money. Once he asked me what I had bought and I showed him a pink blouse from Jeans-Jeans. I also paid off Faisal. Then I bought a bag in the market for 60,000 cedis. I also bought a lock for the bag.

Sometimes when I cooked special food like banku and

okro stew, I saved some for Kwabena Kusi. I could count on finding him at home on Mondays at noon. Once I made him corned beef sandwiches on a Tuesday, but he told me not to come to his apartment unless he sent for me.

"It is so important to keep our secret for now," he said.

I had to be very, very careful.

One Thursday night, I slid into the youth room, late again. Simon looked at me. I smiled but he didn't smile back. Pastor Brown was talking about righteousness.

I rested my head on the back of the pew in front of me. Ellen, a youth worship leader, prayed for all of us to make use of the grace of God to stay pure. Then I realized I didn't want to be in church anymore.

After the meeting, Simon came up to me.

"We have to talk," he said.

So I walked back with him while Jima and Osi went off with some friends. Simon was quiet for most of the walk home.

"Glo, do you want to quit the band?" he asked as we drew near the hospital.

"No," I said. "I have been busy. I thought you were busy with your studies, too."

"I have made some new songs that we have to learn," he said. "Will you come early to youth meeting next week?"

"I'll try hard," I said.

"Good."

We walked on. It felt uncomfortable between us.

"Gloria, are you my girlfriend?" Simon's question surprised me.

"We're good friends, Simon," I said.

"We're more than that," he insisted.

I said nothing.

"So be my girlfriend."

"Oh, Simon, let's just be really good friends," I said. "Best friends."

I took Simon's hand but he made no effort to hold onto mine. We walked in silence for a while.

"Why, Gloria? What has happened?" he asked, freeing his hand.

"Oh, Simon, it's complicated," I said.

"Okay," he said after a while. "Whatever you want."

We didn't stop at the kelewele seller, although I could smell the pepper and ginger in the air. There would be no more kisses in the shadows or his friendly arm around my shoulder. In the moonlight, Simon's smile was small and sad.

• SIXTEEN •

Agnes moved into Dr. Joe's apartment, and all the men doctors called her madam. Her belly was showing a small bulge in her dress. Joe sometimes went to the clubhouse but he never went with her. Then his laughter began to swell once more around the tennis courts.

Sam and I still went for drinks at the clubhouse. Sometimes we met Bea there. She told me the barman liked her and gave her free drinks.

Bea talked a lot about the end of term and her coming party. We went to her house once when her mother wasn't home. She showed me her dress. It was a silky white dress with buttons down her back and a square neckline. It was gorgeous, perfectly matching the shoes and bag she had bought from Faisal.

"Did your daddy buy those?" I asked.

"I bought them myself but he gave me the money."

"You're lucky," I said.

She told me about the Adaekese, the biggest festival of the Ashanti. This year it was falling on the first week of December, and Daddy Lumba, Kwadwo Antwi, Akosua

Adjepong and Stella Dugan were being featured on the main stage. Lord Kenya was also releasing his new hip-life album, *Nsoromma*.

"You can't miss this, Glo. Even if I have to run away from home, I'm going," said Bea.

On Thursday, I got to the church early for practice, as Kwabena Kusi was on duty at the hospital. We practiced until five-thirty. Then Ellen, the other worship leader, came to say hi. Like me, she loved to sing, and she was taking remedial courses for failed JSS courses.

"I thought I was leading today," she said, when she saw me with the microphone.

Osi said, "Gloria's leading today. Pastor Brown changed the schedule around."

"Ellen, we could both lead," I said. "That should be fun."

Our two voices were so much more powerful, and we found that we worked very well together.

"We should do this more often," said Ellen happily.

I was enjoying it so much that I thought I'd ask Simon about having Ellen in our band. Bea had not practiced with us since our show at the cultural center, and she no longer attended our youth meetings.

Ellen was so direct and open. She hadn't hidden her poor exam results but had asked for my prayers. She was going to do the exams again and was hoping to do better the next time. I never spoke of my failed exams.

When it was time to start the meeting, Osi gave the welcome and handed the microphone over to me. I called us all to stand and began to lead the praises. Soon we were lost in the wonder of the music. Sometimes I led the singing, at other times Ellen took the lead. My voice was lower and so I sang the alto parts. Ellen's was a high soprano.

Then at six-thirty, Pastor Brown walked in with Julie, Christine and Sam. Sam was riding on Christine's hip.

What a surprise! I would have been in so much trouble with Christine if I had gone to the hotel first, as I always arrived at church after seven o'clock.

Pastor Brown made the announcements and the introductions. We were told the meeting was a special one and that we were very fortunate to receive Dr. Julie Otoo who was going to tell us about AIDS.

Julie took the microphone. Then she greeted us, acknowledging the pastor, Christine, Sam and me. Everyone looked at me.

We listened to Julie as she began to tell us about the illness called AIDS. I wished Bea had come, too. How little we knew, I thought, as Julie explained about viruses. Without a blood test, it was impossible to tell who was infected. Anyone could have the virus if they had come in contact with infected body fluids through sex or transfusions, and not even know it.

"As we speak, some people are infecting their loved ones through sex because they don't even know they have the HIV virus. And young people are at the greatest risk because they are sexually active and not usually in committed relationships."

Suddenly I became afraid for my sister Effie and Bea. At least Kwabena Kusi used condoms. Besides, doctors would know better.

I learned that the virus attacked disease-fighting cells. Worst of all, there was still no cure. The medicines that could help were only to be found in Europe and North America.

"They are too expensive for Ghanaian pockets," Julie said. "That's the tragedy of it. But a greater tragedy is that we don't talk about it, we don't admit to it. People blame witches and curses when all along it is an illness that has spread because of behavior and ignorance. And what do we do once we know this? What can you do to protect yourself?"

Ellen put up her hand. "We can choose not to have sex before we marry."

The audience stirred as people whispered one to another.

"Yes. The Bible tells you to wait till you're married. But some people won't wait. This is a fact. So if you must, then you have to protect yourselves by having the male wear a condom. It's the easiest thing to do."

I didn't dare look at Pastor Brown. In fact, I couldn't look at anybody. Dr. Julie tore open a plastic package and unrolled a condom sheath.

"A man wears a condom on his penis, and this protects himself and his partner from unwanted pregnancy. If the pastor's preaching is being adhered to, you won't need this until you marry, but just in case there are some among you struggling with sex, this is what you do or insist on."

The room was so silent, I could hear not only mine but Simon's breathing close at hand. We all sat there, our questions in our minds, and yet we couldn't find the words or courage to speak up.

Christine said, "I have an idea. Why don't you each take a piece of paper and write a question or a comment. Don't write your name. Just place your question in the offering box when it comes to you, and Julie will answer them."

A few people began scribbling.

"Everybody has to write something," Julie said. "Only Sam is excluded."

Our laughter broke the tense silence. After a few minutes Ellen took the offering bowl around.

Dr. Julie began to read the questions out aloud.

"Can you get the disease if you share the same glass with an infected person? No. But we ought to be careful of sharing the same glass because many illnesses are passed by that kind of contact."

Julie read off another piece of paper. "Can you get the illness through tongue-to-tongue kissing?" A hum of embarrassment passed through the audience. We were not used to talking about such things in the presence of adults, especially in church. There were other questions about pregnancy and abortion — questions that I thought about sometimes and had no one to ask.

Dr. Julie answered them all.

We cheered and cheered after the speech. I was doubly proud for knowing the doctors, although I worried about what I had learned that evening.

If doctors knew this much, why had Joe got Agnes pregnant?

•

All of Kumasi turned out to celebrate with their king, the Asantehene, at the cultural center where he sat in state. Kumasi was full of splendidly dressed people. We found good seats in the shade of a large canopy because I was in the company of doctors of Komfo Anokye Hospital. Christine, Sam and I sat with Julie and Mimi in a large group of doctors.

We watched the procession of chiefs coming to greet and swear oaths to the Asantehene. We saw the dances of the queen mother's entourage, the dances of the traditional militia and the dances of the abrafo, the king's ceremonial executioners. There were the traditional shrine priests and priestesses dusted from head to toe in white as they performed trance-dances to the playing of the drums. I had never seen so many people in my life.

Dr. Joe and some others arrived. They were draped in all kinds of fine cloth and they went around shaking hands. I watched Kwabena Kusi from my place beside Christine. He looked grand in black-and-white Adinkra cloth, one bare shoulder exposed in a handsome manly way. Joe's Agnes followed the men with some of the other ladies, and there was that curly-haired woman again.

I wished I could ask Bea who she was. Bea knew all the nursing students.

I heard the woman's shrill voice, "Kwabena Kusi, *mo ntwen*."

He stopped and waited for her to catch up. Right then, I began to hate her.

When they had done their round of handshaking, they came and found seats in our part of the canopy, and the conversations grew louder. Joe was talking across to Christine and Julie. Mimi was talking to Dr. Singh, a new doctor from India. I watched Agnes. She hardly exchanged any words with Joe but her friends surrounded her and they held their own conversations with much laughter.

The musicians mounted the podium late into the day. They were all there, every one of them, from the old to the young, from the traditional to the contemporary. The entire audience sang along with them. It was a day for people to fall in love. I stole glances at Kwabena Kusi. Once he smiled at me.

Then I saw Bea. She had done her hair in extensions. I was surprised how pretty she was. I wanted to call her but I was sitting with adults. Finally I asked Christine if I could go and buy Fanta for Sam. She took Sam from me and gave me some money.

Bea was radiant in white slacks and a black-and-white strappy spandex top, which showed off her slimness and curves. She stood tall on high heels, holding a white bag and laughing easily. She was standing among a large group of people, and there were foreigners among them. These were people she obviously knew well. To my surprise, I saw Faisal standing next to Bea.

"Bea," I exclaimed.

"Hi, Glo," she said putting her arm around me. She turned to Faisal. "See, I said she was here."

"My friend Gloria," Faisal said, rolling the *r* of my name on his tongue. "You stay here with us?"

"I'm buying drinks for Sam."

"I'll go with you then," said Bea.

We bought the drinks and returned to the canopy. Bea greeted everyone. Christine said we could go off on our own if we wanted.

"I'm sure you'd like to dance to Lord Kenya in front of the stage. Just get home by eight o'clock."

We wandered about the grounds arm in arm and went back to join Bea's friends.

"Sami likes me," Bea confided about the other foreigner who was with Faisal. Sami suggested that we all go to the Lebanon Club for dinner.

"They make the finest kebabs there," Faisal said.

In the end, six of us left for the club. I tried the different-tasting food. The Lebanese ate sugary foods. Bea and I tried beer. Then Bea followed Sami inside, leaving us in the courtyard. Faisal leaned over and put an arm around me.

"You come inside?"

I wriggled out of the circle of his arm. I had pledged my love to someone else, and Julie's talk on AIDS was still on my mind.

"I want to go home," I said.

"I thought we were friends," Faisal said. "Have I not always been good to you?" His eyes did not seem as friendly as in the past. He took my hand in his and I felt the hard nail scrape against my palm. I withdrew my hand and stood up.

"I am going home." I had never been so bold. It was already dark but I knew the area well and it wasn't far from the doctors' flats. Something in me felt so strong for saying no to Faisal. I wished I could have called for Bea, but I didn't dare go inside and I was too shy to shout.

"Ah, Bea, just be careful," I whispered to the wind.

Then, once outside the gates, I ran home.

• SEVENTEEN •

I sat down on the stairs outside our apartment and waited. The hour passed. The others were late coming, and I
was sorry I had left the cultural center with Bea. Probably
Christine and the doctors had gone off to eat somewhere.
I brushed bloodthirsty mosquitoes away from my face.

I heard a car drive down to the carport and stop. I
went out to look. It was Dr. Joe and Agnes. Agnes got out
and Dr. Joe held her hand as they made their way home.
They were becoming man and wife.

I was still standing in the shadows of the carport when
another car came down the driveway. It sounded softer
than Christine's Corolla.

It was the red Passat. It stopped up ahead at E Block
and for a while the doors remained shut. I waited to catch
a glimpse of Kwabena Kusi. Perhaps I would be able to
wait at his place until Christine came home.

Finally the door opened, and I watched as he went
round to the other side of the car. The curly-haired
woman stepped out. She was almost as tall as Kwabena
Kusi. She wrapped her arm around him and kissed him

on the lips, right there in the open, and he stood there and kissed her for the whole world to see.

My heart missed a beat because suddenly I heard it come back so loud and so fast. I wanted to call his name but I didn't. I watched them go on and on as if they could not stop kissing.

I knew then that Kwabena Kusi had told me lies. Everything he had said were lies, and I had believed him.

Clinging to each other they walked away. I couldn't take my eyes off them. I watched until they disappeared into E Block. Then I sat down again, remembering the hotel, remembering Kwabena's words and the softness of his eyes. I remembered the Chinese food, my fufu and groundnut soup and the low purring of the red car that I had come to know so well. My tears fell.

I waited and waited, but they didn't come out. Then the lights in Kwabena Kusi's apartment went out.

•

The Harmattan began in force the next day. I woke up under a gray blanket of dense fog that only lifted after noon, taking the chill away. There was dust in the wind, dust in my nostrils, my eyes and even my mouth if I opened it long enough. I had to oil my skin with Vaseline petroleum jelly and shea butter to keep the moisture in.

I felt angry with Kwabena Kusi. Then I felt sad. Then I felt angry with myself. I looked out for him from our balcony when I hung out the washing, or when Christine sent me out on errands. I sneaked up to his apartment twice and knocked on his door. Nobody answered and I ran back home again.

There were times I saw his Passat in the carport, but it was impossible to go out then.

Sam and I played with his puzzles and his Lego. We watched TV and cartoons but I could not concentrate on the stories. I didn't even listen in when Christine spoke to JB.

All I wanted to do was ask Kwabena Kusi who the curly-haired woman was and why he kissed her. I felt used. I felt stupid. I felt God would never forgive me. Then I thought I deserved it all because I had disobeyed Daa. Sometimes alone in my room, I wept.

Christine asked me if I was sick.

"I miss home," I said. I wished I could tell her about Kwabena Kusi.

"It won't be long until we visit," she said. "Be patient."

I looked for Bea everywhere. She would know the woman. Bea knew everyone.

She was never home, though. She no longer came to our apartment and she didn't come to the clubhouse anymore. I wondered if she was angry with me for leaving her at the Lebanon Club that night.

In the evenings I tried to read my books and do my grammar exercises. Christine tested me in spelling. She seemed pleased at my progress.

I missed Effie badly. She would have understood. I even tried to write her a letter, but it was difficult. I thought often of Daa and Maa. Daa had been right about steering clear of boy-matter, but he wasn't right that boys didn't make good friends to girls. Simon was a good friend.

The next Tuesday I was out walking with Sam when I saw Kwabena Kusi driving home. I stopped by the side of the driveway. His car stopped by me and his window came down.

"Hello, Gloria, I've missed you," he said.

My heart still jumped at his words.

"On Thursday I'll pick you up as usual, hmm?"

I stared as he waved, and slowly his car rolled on. I hadn't been able to say a word!

I began to plan for Thursday. I rehearsed everything I wanted to say. I would tell him what I had seen that Saturday night. He would have to explain everything. He would have to choose between that woman and me.

Thursday came and all day I felt uneasy in my belly. I wore a green dress that Christine had given me. I powdered my face carefully and applied black kohl around my eyes. Then I used lip gloss to make my lips shine. I wanted to look my best.

In the evening, I set out on my way to church. I walked slowly, watching for the red Passat, but Kwabena Kusi never came. I walked all the way to the church and then I understood that I wasn't important to Kwabena Kusi at all. It was truly over and my heart was broken.

At the church Ellen joined our band, and we began to practice Christmas songs. I wasn't feeling well so I sat out and watched them. They laughed a lot together. Simon said our band would be performing at the youth Christmas service. I wondered if Simon liked Ellen as he had once liked me.

At home, we prepared for JB. Christine stocked the cupboards and ordered special cakes, but she didn't buy any biscuits. She said JB would bring them from the UK, as the English made the very best biscuits of all. She stopped arguing with him on the phone. She bought a new tablecloth and new sheets. She said that we would return to Accra with JB for Christmas.

One evening, Mimi brought Christine news that Kwabena Kusi and Carla had gone to Accra. He was going to perform the customary knocking for permission to marry Carla. Perhaps their wedding would follow in January.

That was how I learned the name of the curly-haired woman and found out that she was a dentist.

That night, in my bed, I cried and cried. How did I, a house-help, compare to a woman like Carla? I felt very foolish and dirty. I hurt badly inside but I couldn't tell anyone about it.

Oh, how I missed Effie.

•

I worked harder than ever to keep my mind off things. I cleaned every room in the house and even scrubbed the floors. On Saturday I went to the market and cooked.

I was reading on my bed on Sunday evening when Christine called, "Gloria!"

Her tone had enough edge to have me jump out of bed. I wondered if something had happened to Sam. Christine looked sterner than I had ever seen her.

"I am missing some money. I had it in my drawer inside my wardrobe and I haven't checked on it for at least two months. It's English money. Pounds sterling."

"Sistah, I haven't seen it," I said.

She looked me directly in the eyes for a long moment. "I'll look again," she said.

"Do you want me to help you look for it?"

"No, thanks. Let's just hope I find it."

I returned to my room and prayed. I had taken her make-up sometimes, and her shampoo. Sometimes I spent a bit of the shopping money on sweets for Sam and me, but I had never taken money that she had not given to me.

In D4, the atmosphere turned chilly. After four hours of searching through every drawer, Christine hadn't said a word.

I knew she suspected me. I waited till she had gone off to work the next morning and then I went to her bedroom. My intention was to take everything out of her closet and put it all back one by one. The money had to be there.

For the first time she had locked her closet. I sat on the bed and wept. Sam came up to me.

"Go-go, sssh, don't cry," he said.

Christine took Julie and Mimi to her bedroom when

they came home after work. She must have told them about her missing money, because Julie didn't ask me what I was making for supper, and the look Mimi gave me was grave. Christine shut the door behind her.

After a while even Sam left me and went to search for his mother. He was just tall enough to tip the door handle and open the door, but he couldn't close it behind him. The sounds of voices wafted out.

"It doesn't seem to matter that you treat these girls well. They will always steal or do something that confounds," said Mimi.

"We don't know for sure that she stole," said Julie.

"Where else could the money have gone? The whole envelope is missing. Only that particular envelope is gone and no one has broken in," said Christine.

"Perhaps you put it in some other place," said Julie. "I misplace things sometimes when I'm trying to hide them."

"I wasn't trying to hide it. I just put it where I always keep my money," said Christine. "Listen, I don't want to believe she stole it, but the money's gone for sure."

"But she denies it," said Julie.

"Do you expect her to own up?" Mimi laughed. "This kind of thing has happened to my mother before, so it doesn't surprise me. You should have been more careful, Christine. You're too trusting."

"I guess so. But I thought she was so transparent, even child-like in her ways."

"Hoongh! Nobody is a child in Ghana these days. You'd be surprised what even Sam knows," said Mimi.

"There, you're quite right," said Julie. "All the same I'd rather give Glo the benefit of the doubt."

"Then leave *your* money on the dresser," said Mimi sarcastically.

They all laughed, and tears filled my eyes.

"What are you going to do?" asked Julie.

"I'll ask her again. I hope she tells me the truth. It's not just about the money but also about trust. You have to be able to trust the person who looks after your child."

"If she doesn't own up what will you do?" asked Mimi.

"I'll have to let her go. I don't see any other choice," said Christine.

"Oh! And she's such a good cook," said Julie.

"It's not only about her cooking. I really like her. This is so disappointing. I haven't even been able to speak to her all day," said Christine.

I was trying to finish my chores while this conversation continued. I wondered why they couldn't believe me. Then I remembered that I wasn't always honest. In spite of all the little things I did, I wouldn't steal her money.

Tears came to my eyes. My throat stung. Sam came out again with a CD in his hand, shouting for me. He tripped just outside the door and fell. He let out a loud wail. I rushed to him to pick him up and collided with Christine. She took Sam and turned away from me.

As Julie and Mimi left, Julie swung into the kitchen.

"Glo, you must tell the truth no matter what. I know you go to church. Now more than ever, the truth is important."

"Sistah Julie..." I began, and tears rushed into my eyes.

She held up her hand.

"I don't need to know anything from you. Christine needs to hear the truth," she said. And she left.

I considered owning up even though I hadn't taken the money. Sometimes if one owned up and begged, things blew over quicker. Yet this was something I hadn't done. And I couldn't stand to call myself a thief.

Supper was ready and I fed Sam. I wasn't sure whether to eat, as Christine had not come out to eat nor yet spoken to me. Finally she came out for her supper.

"Gloria, this is your last chance to speak up. I had three hundred pounds sterling in a brown envelope in the third drawer of my closet. Did you take it?"

"Sistah Christine, I swear I didn't take it. I swear on my father, my mother — "

"Stop it," she said. "Don't bring curses down on other people."

"Sistah, if you like we could go to Pastor Brown or even your own pastor and I will swear on a Bible. If I'm lying the Bible will find me out."

"I don't do such things." Then as an afterthought, she said, "Let's look through your things in the closet."

"Okay," I said, and too late realized I had things in my bag that she knew nothing about.

I followed her into the room. She found the old bag with the broken zipper and overturned it on the bed. There were only old clothes in it. Then she looked in the closet and found my new bag. I could imagine what she was thinking as she looked at the blue travel bag stuffed in the corner of my closet.

"Where did you get this bag?" she asked.

"In the market," I said.

"Who gave it to you?"

"I ran an errand for one of the doctors and they gave me twenty thousand cedis."

She noticed the lock.

"Where's the key?"

I fished in my drawer and gave her the key. She opened it.

My books came out first, then Effie's letters. Next came some clothes Christine had given me and the red Diva T-shirt and stretch jeans. There was my glitter belt with the shiny silver buckle. Then some gifts I had bought for my family. There was also another twenty-thousand cedi bill.

"Can you explain these?" she said, picking up the T-shirt and the jeans. "How did you get designer clothes?"

I was quiet.

"Is this what you used my money for?"

"No," I said. "I didn't use your money. I bought the clothes on credit and people gave me money when I ran errands for them."

"And who exactly have you run errands for?"

Again my lips pressed themselves shut.

"Gloria, you disappoint me," said Christine. "JB is coming in a matter of days and when he leaves I will take you to Accra and decide this matter before your parents."

I burst into tears.

"Sistah, I didn't take your money. I would never do that to you," I said between sobs.

But Christine just walked out and left me in my bedroom.

My whole world was coming to an end, one trouble after another. First I had lost Kwabena Kusi and now I was in danger of losing my future.

After that, I walked about like a shadow, silently unless I was alone with Sam. I didn't venture out to the clubhouse or even in the compound because I wasn't sure who knew what had happened. Had Bea heard? What about Kwabena Kusi? He seemed to have disappeared from our compound altogether.

Simon came to see me after the Thursday youth meeting because I had not shown up. He came with Ellen. I told them I had been busy because JB was arriving in the next few days. Simon wanted to play the new song but I could not sing it. There was no joy to sing from.

Finally I told them that Christine had lost some money and that there was trouble at home.

"I don't know what will happen. She doesn't believe that I know nothing about it."

Simon was angry at Christine but Ellen suggested that we pray. I was happy for their company but I didn't want them to stay long because I did not want to get in trouble with Christine. They asked if I had seen Bea.

"Not since the Adaekese Sunday," I said.

"She got into trouble for missing school," Simon said. "She missed school several times with the excuse that she was ill but her teacher saw her in someone's car in town."

"Oh, no!" I said.

"They checked with her mother, but she didn't know anything about Bea's sickness and her many absences from school. They nearly suspended her but instead she was given a large plot to weed and ten lashes in her hand."

It was too bad that both Bea and I were having trouble at the same time. If I had a chance I would go and see her. School would be over for Christmas in just a few days.

Simon left with Ellen. I hoped they would not tell everyone at youth meeting about the lost money. What would Pastor Brown think? All the grown-ups were bound to side with Christine. Julie still talked to me but Mimi gave me the full silent treatment. She was a lot harder than even Christine.

Once in Accra, a teenager had stolen money. Her parents beat her and hung a sign around her neck that said: I am a thief, beat me. Wherever she went people just hit her if they wanted. It was my father who had pleaded for her. "Jesus said the one without sin should throw the first stone," he had preached loudly. My mother said the girl was lucky they hadn't put ginger or pepper in her eyes to punish her. A long time ago that's what was done to thieves, to remove jealousy from their eyes for other people's things.

• EIGHTEEN •

Christine's time off began the next day. She had asked for special permission because her husband was coming. Her mood improved when phone calls came confirming JB's arrival in Accra. Finally she said he was leaving at dawn for Kumasi.

It seemed as though everything was forgotten. She was talking to me again, laughing and keeping busy. I wondered if she had forgiven me.

Julie, Mimi and Joe had gathered in our living room to wait for JB. Whenever they heard a car they rushed to the balcony to look and Sam screamed, "Daddy, Daddy!"

"He probably won't recognize JB. It's been seven months since he saw him," said Mimi.

I knew Sam would recognize his dad. We looked at his photos every day. He would recognize his voice, too. Sam had a tape called a talking letter, and it was a long message from JB. He even read Sam's favorite story on it. *"Not me," said the monkey*. We always played it for Sam before he fell asleep.

We heard a car as it slowed into our carport and

stopped. Everyone rushed to the balcony and Christine screamed. I thought something had happened to her but the man who stepped out of the car waved, and she charged out of the house. She left the door ajar and tore down the stairs.

Julie had Sam in her arms. She pointed to JB and said, "Sam, look, your dad."

"Samuel Antwi Ossei," said Sam's dad, waving hard at Sam.

Then Julie followed Christine downstairs. I went down with the rest of them to help bring JB's bags up. There were three large suitcases and a small bag.

"You must be Gloria," he said.

His voice was a lot deeper than I had heard on the phone. He had eyes that laughed and two dimples in his cheeks. He was clean shaven and wore small rectangular spectacles, giving him a very distinguished look. He seemed so fit and strong like Joe, who worked out and had a flat belly and big muscles.

"I hope you looked after Christine and Sam well because I do have your surprise," he said.

The smile felt foolish on my face. Nobody else said anything and the moment passed.

"I'm Joseph Boakye Ossei," he said, giving me his hand.

His handshake was warm and his voice friendly. He was someone I knew I would like very much. I reached for one bag to carry it, but he stopped me.

"What are you thinking?" he said. Then he turned to his friends and said, "This girl doesn't know that when an

Ashanti man is coming home, only robust men have enough strength to carry the bags." His laughter made us laugh. He picked up a bag, Joe picked up the other and the taxi driver picked up the third bag. We made a single file up the stairs to flat D4.

Once the suitcases were put away, everybody settled in the living room. JB took the couch next to Christine and Sam sat on his lap.

"Everybody, time to leave," said Joe. "The man has missed his wife."

"Not before we work through amanee," said JB.

Christine got up and fetched a bottle of Champagne from the fridge. She told me to bring water and a glass. I poured ice-cold water into a pitcher and set it on the tray with a tall glass. Christine stood on a chair to reach the top shelf of her pantry. She pulled down some thin-stemmed glasses I had never seen her use.

"Rinse these quickly and bring them to me," she said. Then she took my tray to the living room.

I knew all about amanee. Nobody ever came to visit in Accra without my father performing amanee, the story of their visit.

By the time I got back to the living room, JB's news had been received, he had drunk his water and everyone was waiting for the glasses. JB popped the Champagne. Laughter rang out as they poured Champagne and toasted each other.

"Glo, bring your glass," said JB. "This is the one time a teenager may taste alcohol."

So I tasted the drink they called Champagne. It was fizzy and strange. Sam was screaming for a drink so I brought him some ginger ale.

The first few days, it seemed as if all the doctors in Komfo Anokye came to visit. I never knew there were so many. People stayed and talked. JB had so much to tell them. Sometimes he showed them photos. Often people stayed to eat. I was cooking twice as much as I normally cooked. Christine and JB went out together often. They went out with friends, too. Then Sam and I would spend the time playing with his new toys.

He had several new action toy figures: Superman, Spiderman and Batman. It was Batman that he liked the best because he came with a car JB called the Batmobile. Sam had his own toy computer that made sounds and showed pictures and words. I could read those words, too. JB hadn't given me my surprise so I thought Christine must have told him about the money. Or perhaps he was saving the gift for Christmas.

Mostly the feeling at home was good, and I hoped that Christine would believe me and let me stay. I prayed every night. I said to God that I would never do bad again if we could find the money. I said that I had done many wrong things but I promised him that I would do much better, tell the truth and not take a boyfriend until I was ready for marriage.

The next Thursday we set up the Christmas tree. It was a small artificial tree and we decorated it with many shiny bulbs in gold and silver and red. Then we draped silver and gold tinsel all over it. Sam was beside himself with excitement, and we had to stop him from pulling the ornaments off.

I asked Christine if I could go to youth meeting. To my surprise she said yes.

Then in a strict voice she said, "Be good!"

"Why, isn't she good?" JB asked.

It was meant to be a joke, but Christine's silence spoke volumes. I knew she would tell him everything. I prayed all the way to youth meeting.

Practice was okay. I wasn't very happy so I did not have my usual energy. But I sang well and Simon and Ellen were kind to me. I realized that they hadn't told Osi or Jima about Christine's lost money, and I was really grateful for that. I declined to lead the worship for the youth meeting but I allowed myself to rise on the songs that Ellen sang. I began to feel better inside.

On our way home after youth meeting, Simon said, "Glo, have you ever left Bea alone in your sister's room?"

"No. Why?"

"She's been flashing a wad of pound sterling notes around."

"Did you see her?"

"No. But someone I trust said so. She said Bea's dad had given it to her."

"Bea's father is rich," I said. "He's even going to throw a party for her at the clubhouse."

"Everybody knows her father is rich, but she's never had much until recently," said Simon.

"Even if he's rich he'd give her cedis, not pounds sterling," said Ellen. "I don't trust Bea. She has changed a lot."

I didn't say anything. I, too, had changed, except nobody knew what I had done.

"These days she goes around with businessmen, barkeepers and foreigners, and she's always boasting about the party she's going to have. She should have heard the talk on AIDS," said Simon.

"Glo, haven't you ever allowed Bea into your sister's room? Think," said Ellen.

I let my thoughts wander through the months of our friendship.

"Wait a minute," I said. "I let Bea into Sistah Christy's room that day I quarreled with her. We were trying on make-up when the doorbell rang. It was after that Bea quarreled with me and left. That was before the Anansekrom concert."

I remembered that evening well. I had dressed up in the red T-shirt and the blue jeans. That was the first time Kwabena Kusi came to our door.

"Let's go and ask Bea now," I said.

"No," said Ellen. "You'd better tell your sister and she can talk to Bea's mother. Bea will never admit a thing to us. You know how tough she is."

Suddenly it made sense. The blue eyeshadow and the gold glitter eyeshadow that I had seen her wear time and again. She had probably taken those from Christine's things, too. I could barely contain myself as I walked home.

We parted at our usual place.

"Thank you very much," I said. "You may have saved me." And I hugged them both tightly.

Everyone was out when I got home. I sat on my bed wondering how to tell Christine. I wondered what Bea would say about me when she was confronted. I felt very anxious. The moments passed.

I checked the thermos. There was no hot water. JB always made tea before he went to bed. I boiled water and poured it slowly into the flask. Then I went to bed. I heard them come in but it was too late to talk.

Christine opened my door. She was checking on me.

"She's asleep already," she said. "Sometimes I forget she's still a child."

"Yes, she's still a child," said JB. "At sixteen I bet you couldn't have handled the responsibilities she has to handle, looking after a child and a family full time. So don't be so hard on her, hmm."

"I'm not hard on her. Ask anyone. She stole and there's no excuse for that. Even if she'd just told the truth, I would have forgiven her. What bothers me are the lies. It takes a kind of person to insist on lying. How can I trust her with Sam? Will she tell me if Sam takes a bad fall or swallows something accidentally?"

It was hard to listen to all this. I wished I could tell her everything.

So much had happened since July. But the truth could get me into a lot of trouble. Christine had taken the red Diva T-shirt and the jeans the day she searched my things, and I could imagine her waving them at JB.

"Where did she get the money to buy designer clothes?" she asked. "Up until now she has not been able to explain how she got them. The plot thickens, hmm? Maybe she leaves Sam to have affairs."

"Does she get some allowance for herself?" JB persisted.

"No, but I give her money sometimes for treats when she's out with Sam, and she can ask if she needs something."

"What about her pay?"

"I don't pay her. I've taken over her upkeep and future education. I've only recently begun to save for her just in case we have to move to England after all."

"So what is she to do if she finds clothes she wants, or shoes or even sanitary towels?"

"She's a child. I supply her needs just as my parents did when I was her age."

"Christine, you could ask your parents for clothes, but can she ask you?"

"Of course. We are like a family."

"The operative word here is *like*, Christine. This is not her real family. She doesn't have the privileges your dear sister Grace would have if she was living with you."

I listened to the silence between them. I had always thought we were exactly a family, and now I began to understand the difference. I remembered my old fights with Effie. No matter what I did or where I lived, we would always be sisters. But Christine was my sister as long as I pleased her.

"I want to give her the clothes I bought her," JB said.

"No," Christine insisted.

"At least the towel then."

"No!"

"Tomorrow we'll talk to her. I'm sure she'll tell me the truth."

"JB, you think you're so charming, hmm? No one can resist your large eyes and velvet tongue."

I heard their laughter.

I was first to wake up the next morning, and I immediately started on my chores. I swept the house, washed Sam's diapers, washed the bathroom and dusted, all before everyone else woke up.

I started on breakfast. I fried eggs, tomatoes and mushrooms. Then I made the toast. I squeezed ten oranges for fresh juice. JB had completely banned chemicals from the house. But he did enjoy his beer and his wine in the evenings. I did not sit with them for meals as before.

As I brought his marmalade to the table, he told me to take a seat.

I sat down nervously, facing Christine. She did not smile but went straight to the point.

"I have told JB about the money. I showed him your clothes and he wants to ask you your side of things," she said.

Tears came unbidden to my eyes and I began to sob.

"Stop it," said Christine. "We're not interested in your tears, just the truth!"

I got myself together and swallowed my sobs until only my chest heaved. Then I began again.

"Daddy JB, I didn't steal the money," I said. "Once, my friend Bea came here while Sistah Christine was away in Accra. I was tidying her room and Bea joined me in her bedroom. Then the doorbell rang and I left her there. Sistah, I never thought Bea could take anything of yours but yesterday Simon said she has been showing off pounds sterling in school. I have also seen her in blue eyeshadow and gold eyeshadow but I don't know if she took yours or not."

Christine got up at once.

"I thought I had misplaced my make-up. I'll go and look," she said.

"Do you have a boyfriend?" JB asked while Christine was gone.

I couldn't even look at him. I was glad he didn't push it. I was too embarrassed to speak. Then Christine came back.

"I can't find some of my make-up. I'm going to Bea's house. Come with me, Glo."

• NINETEEN •

Christine walked out of D4, her lips pinched shut. I followed her closely, my heart pounding in my ears. Her shoes clipped on the stones as we cut through the bushes and found Bea's home.

Bea's mother was washing clothes outside. We startled her with our greeting. Her hands were dripping with soap suds, and she dried them on the front of her dress.

"Good afternoon, Doctor," she said courteously. "Can I do anything for you?"

"Sister Dartey, we have a matter of some difficulty to discuss," said Christine. "It concerns Bea."

The frown lines on Bea mother's face drew themselves together. Would she get angry and dismiss us? Would she hear us out?

"Come in," she said.

She settled us in the dark living room with the old heavy curtains.

"Water?" she asked.

"No, thank you," said Christine. "Sister Dartey, Bea

and Gloria, here, are very good friends and I am sure you know that Bea comes to our house often."

"Yes. Of course."

"I have lost some money. Three hundred pounds sterling in twenty-pound notes which I kept in my closet," Christine said.

"Oh," Bea's mother gasped. I saw the woman's tense shoulders sag. I felt sorry for her.

"I asked Gloria and she said she has not taken the money. I did not know what to believe. Then we heard from schoolmates of Bea, who are also Gloria's friends, that Bea has been spending money in pounds sterling."

"Bea? Pounds sterling? I don't think so. Doctor, I don't think Bea will steal in spite of the fact that she is sometimes troublesome."

Christine sat still. At last she said, "Sister Dartey, sometimes children get tempted but they are only children and if they do wrong it is important to find out and correct them. It isn't my interest to make a big fuss but if she took the money and she has it, then I'd like it back."

Long moments later, Sister Dartey said, "Excuse me."

We sat waiting in silence. At last she came back. In her hands she held an envelope. She opened the envelope and I gasped.

"There it is," said Christine. "That's my envelope."

Christine counted twelve twenty-pound notes.

"She's spent some of it — sixty pounds," she said. "But at least most of it is here."

"I'm so sorry," said Sister Dartey.

"It's not your fault, Sister, and I have you to thank for even going to look."

"What shall I do now?" Sister Dartey asked. "I do my best for this child, but lately she's giving me so much trouble." There were tears in her eyes.

Christine said, "We should ask her about this money and maybe we'll find out why."

"Please wait," said Sister Dartey. "She said she was going to the clubhouse to buy a drink. I'm sure she's talking to her friends."

While Sister Dartey went out to fetch Bea, Christine and I sat with silence between us. I kept looking at my hands folded one in the other. I was very nervous.

The door opened and there was Bea, surprise in her eyes at seeing us.

"Bea, Dr. Christine wants to talk to you," her mother said.

Bea came and stood tentatively at the doorway. Her mother sat down and sighed. I couldn't look at either of them.

Christine said, "Bea, I lost some money, pounds sterling. Did you take it?"

"No," she said, her voice strong. She turned to her mother. "Mama, I haven't taken anything," she said, her arms open in a wide appeal.

The slap her mother gave her was sudden and shocking. I looked up as Bea gasped. Her hand flew to her face and I shrank into my chair.

"Don't lie," said Sister Dartey. "Don't lie!" Her voice rose, tense and shrill. "Tell her the truth now!"

"But I didn't take the mo — "

The envelope was out of Christine's bag and she was emptying the money on the table.

"There used to be fifteen notes and now there are twelve," Christine said.

"And I found it in your things," said Sister Dartey. "Where are the other three notes, sixty pounds?"

They couldn't get Bea to speak, as much as they tried. Her mother called her bad, wicked and mean and threatened to tell her father.

In all this Bea said nothing. She didn't cry or say anything. Sister Dartey said she'd make Bea pay back the money. Christine said it was okay. Finally Christine thanked Sister Dartey and we left.

Our footsteps were softer on the way home and we didn't speak to each other. I was happy Christine had most of her money back. I hoped she was sorry for accusing me but adults never apologized to children. Besides, it was my fault for allowing Bea into her bedroom.

It was Bea I worried about. What if she took revenge on me and told Christine about Faisal? Then there was the secret party we'd had with Simon and Jima.

Thank God I hadn't told Bea about Kwabena Kusi.

•

Thursday afternoon, I dressed for youth meeting. I knew that Simon and Ellen would be waiting for news about the money and Bea. I wanted to let them know that the problem was solved. I wore my yellow dress with the silver embroidery, the very one I had worn when I first came to Kumasi months ago. I had forgotten all about it for show-your-belly T-shirts and strappy dresses. All it needed was a hot iron to take out the creases.

My hair was still in extensions and a little untidy. I brushed the impossibles away from my hairline and powdered my face. A little kohl pencil brought some definition to my eyes. I did not put on lipstick.

I took a small shoulder bag, big enough to hold my Gideon's New Testament and my hymn book. I set off quickly along the driveway.

I heard the sound of a car purring behind me. I kept walking, refusing to glance back. The car finally came alongside me. It was the red Passat with dark tinted windows. I kept walking. The window slid down.

"Leave me alone," I said.

"Gloria, what's the matter?"

The voice I heard made me freeze.

"Dr. Joe, I didn't know it was you," I said.

"I'm only borrowing Kwabena's car. Kwabena Kusi has been bothering you again, has he?"

I wondered what he knew. Was he truly concerned,

or was he just fishing for information? I said nothing.

Dr. Joe laughed.

"Don't take that man seriously. He's a real playboy," he warned.

Too late, I thought.

"I'm going to town on an errand. I thought you might want a ride."

"No, thanks," I said. I would never sit in that car again.

Dr. Joe stepped on the gas, stirring up red dust. I hurried toward the tro-tro station at the junction. Some of my friends were waiting there. I joined them on the wooden benches of the truck, and we chatted all the way to church as the wind blew gustily through the open sides of the vehicle.

Our practice was excellent, and we discussed the Christmas show the church was putting on. Ellen thought our band's name F Block was rather uninspiring.

"F is what you get when you fail exams," she said. "We need something more positive."

She suggested Abundant Life, but Simon thought it was too Christian. Jima suggested Nu Life. Everyone thought that was cool, especially the way he spelled it. So that afternoon we became Nu Life.

Simon asked about Bea and the money. I told them everything. Ellen thought it was all very sad, but Simon was angry.

"Have you spoken to her since?" he asked.

"No. I haven't even seen her. I think her mother may have put her under house punishment."

We walked all the way from church together. At Bantama, we stopped for kelewele and groundnuts. Then we heard footsteps on the path. Three girls passed by us in a hurry, their slippers slapping hard against the soles of their feet.

"Bea," I called.

She stopped a few feet away. "Who's that?"

"It's me, Gloria."

There was silence.

"What do you want?" Her voice was cool.

"I'm just hoping everything is okay," I said.

"Of course," she replied. Then she ran off to join her friends.

• TWENTY •

I dropped my dishcloth and went to Christine's bedroom when she called me. She was nicely dressed in a floral bareback dress and pink espadrilles. She looked very feminine with her straightened hair tied back in a ponytail. Her make-up was subtle as usual around the eyes, but her lips were a glossy red. She had become more fashionable since JB arrived. I saw the happiness on her face as the sunlight streamed through the window.

JB was at Christine's desk with his back to me. He turned around and said, "Miss Gloria, here's something I brought you."

The gift bag was a swirl of rainbow colors, and it contained a pink bath towel. It was thick and soft just like the one Christine used, but she preferred darker colors — green, blue and red.

"Thank you, Daddy JB," I said and made a curtsy the way I used to for my elementary school teachers.

JB raised an eyebrow, and Christine said nothing.

"Sistah, please thank Daddy for me," I said.

"But you already did so for yourself."

I turned away clutching my bag. At the door I hesitated.

"Yes?" asked Christine.

"Sistah, I am sorry for letting Bea into your room."

"So you should be, Gloria. I treat you like a sister but you should never disrespect my privacy. I was this close to taking you back to your home."

"I'm sorry."

There was the difference right there. One didn't stop being a member of a family for stealing or getting pregnant or any other thing. But I would have been sent away for something I hadn't even done.

There was another bag on the bed, and I wondered if that was the dress I had overheard them discussing. But there was no mention of any other gift. Perhaps that was my punishment, and I deserved it. I resolved to be more conscientious and work harder to do everything just as Christine wanted it.

I remembered Christine's soft fingers rubbing pomade on my scalp, and the day we had baked a cake together, and all those times we had shared with Julie and Mimi at the table. All I wanted was to win back the closeness we had shared. I wanted us to be able to talk and laugh as we once did. I wanted to belong like family, even if there were differences.

•

There were five more days to Christmas. JB had gone for a drive with Sam. I finished reading "The Musicians of

Hamburg." I looked through my Ladybird books and chose "Treasure Island" at Level Ten. I began to read about Jim Hawkins. It felt as though each word had a different flavor. I was actually enjoying reading.

But there was nobody here who could really appreciate my achievement. Not Bea or Simon, or Osi or Jima or Ellen.

It was time to write to Effie. So far I had received four letters from her. I searched in my bag and found them. I began to read.

Why had I found her letters so difficult? It all seemed very easy now.

August 8, 1994

Dear Gloria,

It's been so quiet since you left. Maa has not been well lately. Just a cold, she said. Daa says she's just missing you. She is coughing a lot! The prayers are not healing her. She needs a doctor.

I have a secret. I have a boyfriend. His name is Charles Dodoo. He is a seaman and soon he is returning to sea. He's the person I used to go and see after youth meeting. This is the secret I have been dying to share.

Daa has been made the chief deacon. I wish he would find work. But it's a little easier at home because there are only three of us now. Still, I miss you.

Auntie Ruby had a new consignment of clothes. I selected two pairs of jeans, T-shirts and sneakers. She gave me the sneakers for free. Eno and Asibi want to take Maa to the herbalist but Daa says no fetish business is allowed in our home.

Write soon. Tell me what Kumasi is like.

Effie

I took out the second letter.

September 6, 1994

Dear Gloria,

You didn't say anything in your note. Christine visited. She said you were performing with a band. Eiii! Daa said if you want to sing, join the church choir. Christine brought us provisions. Sugar, tea, Milo, milk, sardines and oats. Everyone was happy. I was glad for Maa's sake. She hasn't been eating well. Christine said you were a good girl and very good with Sam. She says next year she will either make you do the JSS again or put you in vocational school. She told Daa she thought you were smart but Daa said you were never good in school. If she gives you a chance to go to school again, take it.

Effie

P.S. My final catering exams are coming up and I need to buy so many things for my kitchen and table settings. Oh, Gloria, if only Daa worked and had some money! Maybe Auntie Ruby will help. Do you think you could ask Christine?

I opened the third letter, slitting the top with a knife. I hoped Effie had found some money for her exams. Instead of buying bags and clothes, I could have sent her some of Kwabena Kusi's money.

October 8, 1994

Dear Gloria,

Won't you write? Guess what? I have met a rich man. He has promised to pay for all the expenses of my final exams. This means I don't have to worry anymore about buying professional cooking utensils, a complete dinner set and the ingredients for my six course dinner. He is very good to me. The only problem is that he is already married. It is all so complicated. How did your concert go? Daa hopes you still go to prayer meeting. Maa says be good. She says it is God who has blessed you with Dr. Christine for a guardian. I think you are so lucky. Write soon.

Effie

And then there was one final letter.

November 5, 1994

Dear Gloria,

Maa's sickness has returned. She is so thin. She must have eaten something bad. She always has diarrhea. We went to see a doctor at Korle-bu. He gave her so many different pills but Maa has not improved.

I broke up with Charles. He said Maa has AIDS. Nobody has explained Maa's sickness. Daa says it is witchcraft. Maybe Dr. Christine can help. Ask her to come and visit. Tell her Maa is very sick.

Effie

P.S. I have found a job at Grace's Rest House as a caterer. Now I actually earn some money and I can pay for some of Maa's medicine.

I sat still with the last letter in my hand.

I was filled with horror. My maa was dying. Why had I been too proud to ask someone to read my letters for me?

I knocked on Christine's door. She was lying on her bed reading.

"Sistah, my maa is sick," I said. And I showed her the letter. She read it in seconds.

"Oh, Gloria," she said.

"I just opened the letter. I was waiting to read well first." Then I burst into tears.

"Ssh, Gloria, don't cry. I'll call Accra right away."

Christine called her mother and I held back my sobs as I heard her make arrangements to have my mother taken to Korle-bu Hospital. Then she made another call to her doctor friend at Korle-bu.

That evening, to take my mind off Maa, JB brought out his photos.

"Gloria, come and see my pictures of London. Who would not want to live here?" he asked.

Christine rolled her eyes at him. I said nothing.

London was old. There were rows of brick houses, narrow roads and people in jackets and scarves.

Where were the tall shiny buildings, I wondered. The houses were small and crowded, not like the large houses in Labone Estates where I had first visited Christine. Only the parks were lovely, and the flower gardens were beautiful.

"My plan is to take you there, so long as Christine comes," he said, trying to make me laugh.

"Would you take me? Oh, Sistah, please say yes," I implored.

"Say yes," said JB.

"Yes, yes," said Sam, who had no idea what was being said. Superman was in his hand and he was swooping about the room with a piece of cloth tied to his back. Sam had given his affection over to Superman ever since he had watched the cartoons JB brought. Batman with his Batmobile was already out of fashion.

"Oh, all right," said Christine, and JB engulfed her in his arms.

Sam pleaded, "Me too, me too, me too!"

They allowed him in for a hug.

I watched them from my place by the coffee table, one happy family.

•

The wind rushed over my face as Daddy JB drove Christine's Corolla to Accra. So much had happened in six months in Kumasi and at last we were returning for a visit. Inside the car Christine passed sandwiches around and we drank our Sprite out of bottles.

Just before Konongo, I recognized the turning into the rest house I had visited with Kwabena Kusi. We did not stop there.

We drove past bush and small scattered villages. There were vendors at the roadside holding up bunches of large mushrooms, the occasional bush rat and buckets of large forest snails. I saw children following their parents into the bush to farm.

JB drove fast. Sam fell asleep. At Nsawam, we stopped to buy huge soft loaves of sugar bread for our relatives in Accra. The vendors pushed boiled eggs at us through the windows.

It was in Nsawam that we fell into the worst traffic. The sun beat down on us hard, making Christine's air-conditioning useless. We traveled in silence, thankful that Sam continued to sleep. Bit by bit, we approached Accra. We edged past the guards at the police barrier and mingled with the heavy city traffic.

I watched Accra through the rolled-up glass of my window. I had walked my part of it to school and back, playing in the neighborhoods, selling oranges along its streets, shopping in the markets and running errands. I watched Accra with the eyes of a newcomer.

We stopped first at my home in Alajo. Only Maa was home. She had lost weight, her face was weary, her eyes tired and her voice had grown softer. I went to her and hugged her.

"*Atuu!* It's so good to see you, Gloria. How you have grown."

Maa brought us water to drink. She filled three glasses and set them on a tray. I was amused that she treated me like a guest.

Christine and JB stayed for a while. Sam clung to Christine. They asked Maa about her health and looked at her medications. They seemed quite satisfied that Maa was feeling better.

Then JB handed Maa an envelope. "Your Christmas gift, Mama."

"You shouldn't have," said Maa.

"Please," JB insisted. "We are so lucky to have Gloria."

Maa took the envelope. At the car, JB gave me some money, too.

"For you and your sister," he said. "We will see you on Christmas day."

"Thank you, Daddy JB," I said. "Is Maa really okay? Will she live?"

"Gloria, I think she is feeling better," said Christine, and she gave me a hug with her free arm.

"It's in God's hands," said JB.

Nobody wanted to discuss Maa's illness. It seemed to me that everyone hoped that it would simply go away.

Eno and Asibi were extracting palm oil in a ten-gallon pot. They looked hot and sweaty. James Adama sat in the shade of the mango tree repairing shoes.

I looked at the shabby compound, the broken chairs on the veranda, the crooked aluminum shack we called a bathroom with the bath water draining slowly in the cement-lined gutter. The little children playing in the yard were dirty, their clothes too big or just absent. Their toys were broken pieces of other people's garbage. Even when they cried, the sound was different than I heard from Sam — coarse, tight and wretched.

Effie came home carrying a plastic bag in each hand. She was in her white caterer's dress, with wide lapels and white buttons running down the front and two large pockets.

She dropped her bags and ran to me and squeezed me in a big hug. She was looking older. She had deep blue eyeshadow wide around her eyes, black kohl eyeliner thickly spread on the edges of her lids and a deep purple lipstick.

Then we were back in the same room we had shared. The room seemed smaller. I put my bags on the floor by the wall and we sat on the bed just as we'd always done. Effie and I broke chunks off the sugar bread to eat.

"Blue Band?" she asked, pointing to the can of margarine on the table.

I shook my head. I was used to the more pleasant taste of Planta margarine.

"You're looking different," I said.

"It's my hair. I permed it."

"And you've got on a lot of make-up. How does Daa feel about that?"

"I guess he realized I was no longer a child. After all, I bring home the money," she said with a chuckle.

"Effie!"

"It's the truth," she insisted. "Gloria, I'm so glad you're back. You only wrote once, so you must boss me everything."

I told her about Christine, Sam and JB. I told her about Bea, Simon, Dr. Joe and Julie. I told her about F Block and Nu Life. I told her about Pastor Brown and about the theft.

"Oh, Gloria, that girl Bea is bad," said Effie.

"She's not all bad. She just wants nice things, too." For the first time I told someone about Kwabena Kusi and how he had lied to me.

"He was *bad*," I said.

"Ah, Gloria, you're a big girl now. I wish you were not so far away," said Effie. "Then I could watch out for you."

She told me how she had broken up with Charles. She also told me about Mr. Otoo, the rich man who had a wife.

"Effie, you must break up with him," I said. "It's wrong. He's lying to you and besides, we have to be so careful about AIDS."

I told her about Dr. Julie's talk.

She shrugged. "You're lucky. Someone takes care of

you. I have to take care of Maa and Daa, and my job is just not enough."

I told Effie I would try to help more. I would send her all the money I got.

"Effie, things will change. I may be moving to England with Sam and Christine to join JB next year," I whispered.

She screamed with delight. "If you get there, work hard and send me a ticket, too."

"Of course," I said.

I heard Maa cough in the other room.

"Effie, do you think Maa has AIDS?" I whispered. "Maa has to take the test."

"No. She's feeling better now that she is taking medicine. She'll soon be her old self again."

Once I had heard on the radio about a woman who had been abandoned by her family because she had AIDS. We were all too ashamed of AIDS to even talk about it. If Maa had AIDS, what about Daa?

Daa came home later with the sunset. He looked the same as before. He was very happy to see me and he asked all sorts of questions about living in Kumasi. But he didn't talk about Maa's illness.

Daa was lucky. He could push away his worries.

• TWENTY-ONE •

Christmas day was hot and dry and spilling over with joy. On the streets, wave after wave of masquerades were performed, frightening the little children. I wondered what masks, costumes and drums had to do with Christmas. Daa said it was the way non-Christians celebrated Christmas.

Our church was full to overflowing. Even people who never went to church attended services on Christmas day, and we spent the entire morning singing praise songs in Ga, Twi and English. We heard the Christmas story again. We raised a hearty collection, dancing through the aisles to deliver our gifts to God. The band rocked and I couldn't stop dancing and waving my white handkerchief.

Then, after the service, we shared cake and soft drinks and cookies. We were all so happy.

The children made long necklaces of Huntley and Palmers gem biscuits. When I was younger I would eat those biscuits one at a time until my piece of thread was bare. Never mind that the biscuits hung around my sweaty neck all day.

After church we rode in Auntie Ruby's taxi, all of us jammed in tight, all the way to the house in Labone where I had first met Christine. The party lasted all day long with music and dancing and tables laden with dishes of rice, fufu, soups and stews. Sam was king, and much too excited to sit down. I met Christine's family and their friends.

Christine and JB had a gift for me.

While Effie watched, I peeled off the sticky tape. If I was careful I could use the shiny wrapper again.

Here was the surprise beyond my dreams: a three-piece outfit in blue and silver with shoes to match. I tried on the jacket. Effie's eyes were bright with happiness.

"Gloria, you are so lucky," she said.

●

We returned to Kumasi a little sad, with JB gone. I promised Effie that I would write her whether I had the right spellings for my words or not. I didn't hide my tears.

"I'll come and visit you in Kumasi," she said. "I promise."

Christine told my daa that she had opened an account for me and was paying me monthly, although I was only allowed a small allowance to spend. Daa protested hard that he had given me as a sister, not as a worker, but he wasn't able to dissuade Christine.

I was glad. I would be able to send some money home.

Christine started the car and off we sped out of the big city. Effie waved hard until we were out of sight.

It was quiet in the car. Sam slept and I thought about Maa, Daa and Effie — my family. Christine must have been thinking of JB.

"Sistah?"

"Yes?"

I was speaking to the back of her head as she focused on the road ahead.

"I'll take my JSS exams again, as you suggested."

"Smart girl," she said. "It's not the only way forward in life, but it is the best way forward."

Christine turned the knob on the radio and Nana Tuffuor's soulful tenor told of the hardships of life abroad, broken dreams and broken families. The sound of the guitar reminded me of Simon. I couldn't wait to go back to Nu Life practices.

We stopped at the Block D carport just as it turned dark.

The trunk was full of food: yams, plantains, tinned milk, sugar, sardines and corned beef. Christine's mother had done a lot of shopping for us. It was almost as if there was no food in Kumasi. I grabbed our travel bags first, and with one in each hand, I began up the stairs to our home.

I was making tea and arranging biscuits on a plate when the doorbell rang. I smiled. Julie and Mimi would have seen the lights on in our apartment.

I was right. It was Julie at the door. But instead of a shout of welcome, she looked at me for a long moment as if she was going to cry. Then she reached for me and hugged me tight.

"Oh, Gloria, I'm so sorry," she said.

"What's wrong?"

"Haven't you heard?"

I shook my head, panic starting in my chest.

"It's Bea."

●

We attended Bea's funeral after the first week of the New Year. Nu Life sang at the funeral. I still could not believe that I would never again see Bea walk up the driveway to the clubhouse, or share a taxi from the market.

Sister Janet Dartey's eyes were red from weeping, and those who stood close to her supported her on either side. Dr. Kotoh stood with his head bowed the whole time. His pretty wife, Mrs. Kotoh, the tennis player, stood by him, holding his hand. Even their three boys were there in church. Bea had never mentioned her half-brothers. There were several doctors and nurses and staff from the hospital. Even the clubhouse staff were there, and Bea's friends and teachers from school.

Bea had died from a botched abortion. People said how sad it was, since her father was a doctor and her mother a nurse.

"Too bad," they said over and over.

"Children — these days there is no controlling them," I heard one of Bea's teachers murmur. "They are crazy for the fast life."

"It's all those TV shows from America," a man said. "Too much sex and quick fix wealth."

I looked at Simon. He looked at me and raised his eyebrows.

But it wasn't really Bea's fault, I wanted to say. Her dad never cared about her, never listened to her or even provided for her. Bea was smart, she was fearless. She wanted to be a doctor.

I thought of Bea bearing the burden of a pregnancy by herself. I would have been so scared. Only Bea was bold enough to take all those tough decisions by herself to try to end the pregnancy. She had chosen a cheap quack in order to keep it secret.

The quack had disappeared and the police had not yet found him. Bea had been failed by so many people yet she alone was blamed for her death. Poor Bea.

But I said nothing. No adult was interested in what I thought. In their eyes I was a Nobody.

Christine came round to my side. She put her arm around me and squeezed me.

"Gloria," she whispered. "No more secrets from now on, okay?"

Tears sprang to my eyes. One day I would tell her about Kwabena Kusi.

"No more secrets," I said. And I put my face into her shoulder and wept.

• EPILOGUE •

I am walking down the Bantama Road and the wind is pushing me along. It is the last day of school, JSS3, and my cream and brown uniform has a bit more style than usual because I have pinched the waist a little and shortened my sleeves.

I am walking with a bounce in my step because I have just received the results of the exams. I have passed everything. Everything! I laugh out loud.

As I cross the road into the junior doctors' complex, someone honks and I turn around. A car passes by. It is a red Passat.

"Tschew!" He's not worth my spit on the ground.

I see Sam waiting on the balcony. I see him first but I wait until he sees me, so he can shout, "Glo-glo!" He has returned from day nursery, where he is being taught the alphabet. Sam knows everything. He watches Sesame Street on video.

"Hi, Sam," I shout.

He is speaking quite well in Twi and beginning to speak in English.

"Hi, Glo."

He expects us to keep shouting greetings until I can pick him up and swing him around and around. He is still the cutest and most popular baby in the complex.

Ellen is my best friend and we have helped each other study. Simon has been very busy with his final school exams so Nu Life has been suspended for a while. Effie and I write to each other all the time. She says Maa's health has improved on special new drugs, and Daa is still searching for a job. Christine says she is not ready to move to the UK yet, and JB calls all the time. He will be coming home this summer and has promised to bring me a gift.

I can't wait. Oh, I can't wait!

• GLOSSARY •

Abayifo Witches and wizards.

Abrafo Ceremonial executioners.

Acheampong A particularly hardy weed and also the name of an ex-military Ghanaian head of state.

Achimota A suburb of Accra.

Adaekese An important Ashanti festival.

Adinkra cloth Cloth printed with symbols used by the Akan people of Ghana.

Agushie Melon seeds.

Akpeteshie Strong home-brewed alcoholic drink.

Akutu wula Orange seller.

Amanee A traditional exchange of news when a visitor arrives.

Ampesi Boiled mix of plantain, cocoyam and yam.

Anago Nigerian.

Ananse Guide Ghanaian Girl Guide.

Anansekrom A celebration of music, named after the folklore character Ananse.

Apantu A kind of plantain preferred for making fufu.

Asantehene King of the Asante.

Ashanti Pertaining to the Asante people and their land.

Atuu A welcome hug.

Banku Fermented corn flour dumpling.

Boss Tell a tale, gossip or news.

Boys' quarters An outhouse for servants.

Bubu Long African gown.

Buulu Fool.

Cedi Ghanaian monetary unit.

Chi-bom Egg and vegetable omelet.

Chop-bar A small informal restaurant.

Colo Old-fashioned (from the word colonial).

Drop-in A kind of taxi service that drops you off exactly where you want to stop, in contrast to the usual common stops along a road.

Ene And this.

Fufu Balls of pounded and boiled plantain, yam, cocoyam or cassava.

Ga The Ga coastal people and their language.

Gallon A large plastic container for liquids.

Gyae Stop it.

Handwriting A person's cooking.

Harmattan A dusty dry African wind.

Impossibles Short hairs along the hairline, hard to braid along with the rest of the hair.

Jolof rice Rice cooked in tomato-based sauce with meat or chicken and spices.

Kaba-slit A blouse and long skirt sewn in African fabric in contemporary African styles.

Kelewele Spicy fried plantain.

Kenkey Balls of boiled fermented corn dough.

Knocking Engagement ceremony.

KNUST Kwame Nkrumah University of Science and Technology.

Koko Fermented corn porridge.

Kontomire Leafy green vegetable, the color and taste of spinach when boiled.

Koobi Dried salted fish.

Koose Bean cake.

Kra be whe Spectacular.

Kurasi-ni Uncivilized villager.

Langalanga Slim cutlass used for cutting lawns and grass.

Mini sane What is wrong?

Mo ntwen Wait.

Nsee whee Don't ruin anything.

Nsoromma Stars.

Oburoni-wawu Literally, dead white man; term used for second-hand clothing.

Ogyam Remarkable friend.

Okro A vegetable.

Okyeame Spokesperson for a king or chief.

Rubber Plastic container.

Shadda Dress up fashionably; fashionable.

Tolo-beef Salted beef.

Tro-tro Privately owned mini bus that provides public transportation.

Twi Language of the Akan people of Ghana.

Whe yie-o Be very careful.

Wo ye blade You look sharp (like a blade).